Acknowledgements

I want to thank God for the inescapable gift of writing. My gratitude also extends to all of my family and friends whose prayers and words of encouragement carried me through the highs and lows of birthing this labor of love, and propelled me toward the fulfillment of my dream to become a children's book author. Special thanks to my husband, Timothy Jackson, for consistently supporting me over the years; mother, Hattie Turner, aunt, Joyce Chapman, and daughter, Monet Jackson who edited and critiqued my story; cousin, Kea Taylor, for the artistic vision for the book cover; nephew, Aaron Jackson, for the original artistic rendering used to enhance each chapter page; best friend, Donna Cooper, for developing a web presence for this book; and the cover model, Kendrick Lewis, a current senior baseball player attending Cardozo High School whose eyes symbolize moving beyond the challenges of the past to gaze into a brighter future filled with hopes and dreams.

Dedication

This book is dedicated to my father, Benjamin Randolph Turner, the quiet, yet strong force behind the woman I have become. The powerful love he demonstrated to me over the years was not the reflection of the love he received from his own father. It was the Turner men who stepped up to fill the gap where a masculine void in his life existed which brought balance to his teen and young adult life. I thank God for my great grandfather, Frederick Turner, and great uncles Winston Turner, Lloyd (Bump) Turner, and Fred Turner for taking my father into their homes and under their wings; and for my grandmother, Willena Turner, who birthed a male child into a world in 1934, overcame the stigma as a teen mother did the best she could with what she had.

Chapter 1 - A Sad Farewell (January 14, 1952)

The cold frigid wind blew the limbs of the maple

trees that stretched across the street. The last school bell

had rung over 30 minutes ago. The last few small groups

of boys and girls clumped together as they laughed and

horsed around, chasing each other along the dirt path as

they headed home.

"Come on, Benny," Teddy called behind him,

shuffling his short legs in double steps.

It was hard for Teddy to keep up with the other

boys, whose long legs glided in single strides down the

street. Teddy was tripping over his own feet as he tried to

keep pace with his group, while walking backwards to

encourage his best friend, Benny, to catch up.

But today, Benny wanted to be left behind.

"Go ahead, man," Benny yelled back, "I'll meet you

at *Normandy's*."

Benny waved his hand across his chest, and rubbed

the bill of his cap in between his fingers as one of their

secret baseball gestures to assure Teddy that it was okay to

walk ahead without him. Teddy smiled and motioned

back.

The two boys had been best friends since Benny and

his mother, Lena, moved back to live with his grandfather

mid-way through his fourth-grade year at Kelly Miller

Elementary School. Now, both were 14-years old and

about to end eighth grade at Banneker Junior High School.

Teddy, who was known as Theodore by his teachers, had

come to depend on Benny to defend him whenever the

roughneck boys from Southwest, considered the worst section of Washington, DC, would pick on him.

"I just ain't in the mood for no talkin' and laughin' today," Benny muttered to himself.

He kicked up clouds of dust along the dirt-packed walking path. His normal rhythm slowed to barely sliding his feet forward.

"Ha!" he gasped deeply as he shook his head in disbelief.

Now, every other group of middle schoolers including the group that Teddy had joined, were as blurry brown spots bobbing up and down. Today, Benny didn't care that his friend had left him behind. He dragged his pigeon-toed feet along the dirt road leading to his grandfather, Pop-Pop's, house with a trail of dust marking his path. His face was expressionless and nearly perpendicular to the ground. He didn't stop to listen to the loud argument between the older men sitting along the wooden fence as he got closer to the *Normandy's* corner store. It was always the same debate about who would win the next neighborhood fast-pitch softball game.

Benny's mind drifted to the next place that he would call home. Dread raced through his mind as he contemplated the change that was about to take place— living with Unc, his mother's youngest brother, who would have a lot of strict rules for him to follow.

"I sure wish I could trade places with Teddy right now," Benny sighed, "Sittin' down at the kitchen table eating supper with my mom and dad. Asking them to pass me this and pass me that. Talkin' bout what I did today in school and what we're gonna do tomorrow. I'm gonna miss living with Pop-Pop," Benny lamented.

His chest began to burn as his stomach thrashed about. He fumbled through his jacket pocket to pull out a crumpled sheet of paper. It was the letter that Principal Johnston had given him for Pop-Pop.

Dear Mr. Turner,

I have become very concerned with the home situation of your grandson, Benjamin Turner, which seems to lack the necessary adult supervision for a young man his age. Serious consideration needs to be given to removing him from a potentially detrimental environment, and placing him with a family member who is better able to properly take care of him.

Social Services have begun the process of seeking a family member or foster family who can assist in providing supervision for your grandson during your illness.

Sincerely,

Timothy W. Johnston

Principal

Banneker Junior High School

Benny rolled his eyes. After reading the letter he crumpled it into a tight ball and stuffed it back into his pants pocket. Benny looked up to the evening sky and yelled up to the clouds.

"Uh! Detrimental? What is *detrimental* about living with Pop-Pop? He loves me! I guess that word must have meant a lot to old Principal Johnston, because he sent Miss Ward, the social worker from the school, to visit Pop-Pop yesterday morning while I was at school. She just had to write up that report telling Pop-Pop that if he couldn't find another relative to take care of me; I'd be put into foster care!" Benny snapped.

The sun was beginning to play its own version of hide and seek as it dropped behind the *Washington Star* newspaper building.

"Extra, extra, read all about it! Benny Turner's moving for the umpteenth time!" Benny yelled.

Looking up at the tall beige concrete building, he released a loud sigh and continued the conversation with himself.

"Who's gonna rub down Pop-Pop's feet with Witch Hazel at night? And who's gonna talk to him until he drifts off to sleep, or run to the store to get him a Rock Creek ginger ale?

Unc won't let me keep the change to buy a bag of potato chips or a couple of pieces of *Mary Jane* candy. He'll only make me put any extra change into a piggy bank for my college savings. I don't even know if I *want to go to college!*"

Benny shook his head as he suddenly thought about the stories that he heard about what happens to teenage boys in foster care.

"Shoot, my caramel-colored skin, thin body, and my peanut-size head would make me a target for getting beat up every day for sure! I can see myself now fighting some big bruiser cat that made fun of me." Benny continued to mutter under his breath as his pace accelerated.

"Teddy said that foster care is the worst place in the world for a Black boy to wind up, especially a boy who'll be 15 this year! He always seems to know about bad stuff that happens to kids. Why won't Mama just stay with Pop-Pop or get a place so I can stay with her?" he shouted as he walked the last block to First Street, which led to Pop-Pop's house.

"I'm tired of this! I hate her!" he blurted out loudly.

He didn't care if any of the neighbors heard him and reported his outburst to Pop-Pop. There was an unspoken code of conduct in the Southwest neighborhood that every child understood and that was you never disrespected an adult, no matter who they were or what they had done to you.

Benny began to feel the burning sensation in his chest again as he envisioned himself packing his clothes and all of his belongings into Pop-Pop's worn out dull green colored World War II army duffle bag. Pop-Pop had already told him that if anything ever happened to him, he could have it.

"*Unforgettable... that's what you are . . .*" Nat King Cole's mellow voice danced across the dirt road. It fell upon Benny's ears as it flowed through the tiny transistor radio sitting in the window of one of the neighbor's houses. This time Benny resisted the temptation to imitate his favorite singer with his imaginary microphone and a spontaneous dance move.

"*Unforgettable* is right, Nat. This day is one day that I want to forget," Benny snapped.

The pain of leaving Pop-Pop boiled within Benny's chest. The palms of his hands began to perspire. The burning sensation in his chest now caused his mouth to water as the cheese toast and milk from lunch began to work their way up into his throat.

Pretty soon his feet were kicking up a trail of dirt behind him as he cupped his hands over his mouth. The tears that had been locked beneath his eyelids for the ten blocks of his journey burst forth, cascading down his thin cheeks.

As he drew closer to Pop-Pop's house, he could hear the group of chickens running through the yard. But this time he ignored them as they ran in wild circles across the yard and right across his path –

"*Cack! Cack! Cack! Cack! Cack!*"

He knocked over the bucket of chicken feed as he sprinted up the twenty concrete steps leading to the front door of Pop-Pop's house. He barely made it to the toilet when sour bits of cheese toast forced his mouth wide open.

Uncontrollable gags and gasps awakened Pop-Pop in the rear bedroom.

"Benjamin, is that you?" Pop-Pop called to Benny in a whisper.

As soon as he caught his breath, he shuffled his feet over the worn wooden floorboards leading toward Pop-Pop's bedroom; wiping his face with his shirttail to keep Pop-Pop from seeing that he had been crying.

"Come here, Benny, sit here," Pop-Pop patted a spot on the worn bumpy white cotton blanket.

Pop-Pop was nothing but a thin line of bones hidden underneath the heavy rough blanket. His beige-colored skin dangled loosely from his body. Looking into his large sunken eyes was as if staring at the face of a raccoon. The large dark circles and white whiskers almost dominated his face. His high cheekbones, arrow straight nose, and straight grey hair resembled a noble and respected Indian chief. For a man nearly eighty years old, his mind was still sharp even though he had lost all of his teeth.

He could recall every detail of Benny's life from the time his mother brought him home from the hospital as an infant to the day he was excited about finally graduating from elementary school to attend junior high school.

"Yes, sir," Benny responded, as he continued to wipe the remaining particles of cheese from his chapped lips.

"Are ya okay, son?" Pop-Pop looked into Benny's face.

Benny could smell the sour odor that escaped from his shirt. Pop-Pop slowly turned his head toward where Benny was standing.

"I know the people at the school done told ya that ya gonna have to live with Unc," Pop-Pop said his voice just above a whisper, "And I know ya kinda upset about having to leave from here. But ya know how much I love ya, now don't ya?" Pop-Pop asked.

Benny tried to muster up a strong response, but couldn't get the words to come out of his mouth.

"Ya know that if I could let ya stay here, I would," Pop-Pop's voice cracked as his eyes began to shine like wet glass.

Benny shook his head and faintly responded, "Yes, sir."

"But I'm not as spry as I used to be and can't keep up with ya like I should. Do ya remember when I taught ya how to pitch a fast ball over yonder on Greenleaf ball field?" Pop-Pop asked.

Pop-Pop's eyes widened to make sure he had Benny's attention. Before Benny could respond, Pop-Pop continued to recall the good times that he had with Benny.

"Oh boy! Remember when you *finally* learned how to throw a curve ball?" Pop-Pop asked with a toothless grin.

"Yeah, that was a major accomplishment for me," Benny responded, "I got tired of you telling me –Focus, son, focus, focus, focus!"

Benny allowed a brief chuckle to escape as a faint smile came upon his face.

"And what about the time you pitched a fast one right into Mrs. Dunmore's kitchen window?"

Pop-Pop let out a hoarse chuckle that started one of his coughing spells.

"Yeah, that was funny," Benny interjected with another slight grin.

Benny gently rubbed Pop-Pop's back to calm him down as his mind drifted back to the days when he thought Pop-Pop looked like a giant. His long legs were like stilts in Benny's eyes. And when he threw a baseball, it seemed to cry with a loud shrieking sound as it left his hand and smacked hard into Benny's glove.

Pop-Pop was well respected in Southwest as one of the best ball players in the neighborhood, but he never had the chance to play on one any of the recognized local teams. He would play a pick-up game here and there at family picnics or the neighborhood block party.

"Man, you would have been a great baseball player, Pop-Pop," Benny said with a spark of enthusiasm.

He glanced back at the withered old man who spent most of his life working jobs as a master plumber despite not being able to read. He was determined to support his eight children even if it meant never being able to pursue his dream of playing baseball in the Negro League.

Benny could feel the water levels rising again behind his eyelids, but he tried to hold them back. Pop-

Pop put his cold, thin hand on top of Benny's as he reassured him that he would have a better life with Unc.

"Don't worry about me, son," Pop-Pop whispered.

"But who's gonna take care of you, Pop-Pop?" Benny abruptly interrupted as he allowed a few tears to drip onto the blanket.

"It ain't fair . . .," Benny cried out as his voice began to crack.

Before he could finish his protest, Pop-Pop peeled his thin shoulders away from the wall so he could get closer to Benny's face.

Looking intensely into Benny's sopping wet eyes, he said, "Ain't nothing fair in this world, son -- being Black, being an old man, or being a smart boy like ya'self with no momma and daddy around to take care of ya," Pop-Pop said as if strength suddenly entered his body.

Benny didn't want to blink. He could sense the seriousness of the moment and didn't want Pop-Pop to think he wasn't listening to every word that slipped through his thin cracked lips.

Pop-Pop continued as he leaned even closer toward Benny's face. Benny could feel Pop-Pop's heavy breath bending the fine hairs above his lip.

"Benny, do ya remember the first time that I took ya out into the yard and played catch with ya? Ya barely held on to the baseball, because ya hands were so dog on small," Pop-Pop said.

Benny nodded as he remembered looking up at Pop-Pop as he stood as tall as the Sycamore trees that lined their street.

"Later, ya started playing in the Pee Wee League and then the big boys baseball club. Soon, ya taught me a few tricks about the game." Pop-Pop displayed another wide toothless grin.

"I was so proud of ya, son," he continued.

Benny mustered up a brief, "Yeah," slowly shaking his head in agreement.

Pop-Pop continued talking as he struggled to maintain eye contact with Benny.

"Ya practiced hard to become one of the best pitchers in ya league and I'm proud of ya. Ya never let things get to ya, and I don't want ya to start now," Pop-Pop stated firmly stretching his eyes as wide as he could.

Benny repositioned himself on the bed to move even closer to Pop-Pop.

"Ya know Pop-Pop's getting weak. But I've lived a long and happy life. I need to make sure ya have a happy life, too. So, try to do more with ya life than I had the chance to do with mine. I know things with ya momma ain't that good right now, and who knows where ya daddy is. But Unc knows what ya need to get into the books and get ya ready for high school next year," Pop-Pop said.

With his gums in full view, he declared, "Ya 'bout to be a man, Benjamin!"

Benny hadn't thought much about becoming a man, but hearing Pop-Pop say those words made him feel special.

"Just remember, to listen to what Unc tells ya, Pop-Pop continued gasping for breath in between his words.

"He's a good man who knows what's best for ya. Don't ya ever forget that ya got everything ya need inside of ya to *make* life fair," Pop-Pop emphasized.

Just as slowly as Pop-Pop positioned himself forward, he allowed his thin frame to fall back and reconnect with the pile of pillows. His chest quickly rose up and down as if he had just climbed up the stairs.

The chickens stirred up another chorus as they circled the front yard--

"Cack! Cack! Cack! Cack!"

The ruckus in the front yard rudely interrupted Benny's most important moment with Pop-Pop. Benny could hear the engine of a car stop right in front of Pop-Pop's yard. It was Unc.

Benny leaned over toward Pop-Pop, who placed his cold wrinkled hand over Benny's smooth hand.

"Promise to do ya best, now. No matter what happens good or bad," Pop-Pop commanded as he firmly squeezed Benny's hand; his bones rolled across Benny's palm.

"I promise, Pop-Pop," Benny replied with determination in his voice.

"Cack! Cack! Cack! Cack!"

The chickens were running back and forth in the front yard, flapping their wings in a series of false take-offs to avoid being hit by the bright yellow headlights flashing wildly across the side of the Pop-Pop's house. Unc drove up over the mounds of dirt that defined Pop-Pop's front yard.

"Ya better get packin' son, so ya don't keep ya uncle waiting too long," Pop-Pop said slowly closing his eyes for a few seconds at a time in between each word.

"Yes, sir," Benny whispered with a look of confusion about how he should respond -- lean over to kiss Pop-Pop on the cheek or respectfully respond to his last command?

Without a moment to make a decision, he watched as a dark shadow covered the entire doorway leading into Pop-Pop's room. The figure blocked the dingy light of the foyer from fully resting on the top of Benny's forehead.

"Hey, big man," said Unc. His deep voice echoed in the foyer as he stretched his large, rough hand toward Benny.

Turning quickly as if addressing an Army colonel, Benny extended his hand to offer Unc a handshake.

"Hey," Benny responded, without the usual excited greeting that he would normally give Unc.

"I guess I'd better get packin'," Benny quickly followed up before Unc could give his first command. He turned to run up the stairs.

Unc walked over to Pop-Pop, who was now slumped over to one side of the bed. He placed his large hands on Pop-Pop's shoulders to move his body back toward the center of the pile of flattened pillows, and rubbed the top of the blanket to remove the ripples where Benny had been sitting earlier.

"Pop, you know you did the best you could for Benny, but you can't take care of yourself, let alone look after an active teenager," Unc stated.

He adjusted Pop-Pop's night shirt which was pulled toward the left side of his body.

Pop-Pop allowed a stream of tears to run down his face as he listened to Unc describe the plans already made for him.

"The nurse will stop by here in the morning to get you moved to the nursing home across town," Unc continued, "And Bump and I will take care of packing your things."

Benny stopped moving when he heard the deep bass of Unc's voice bouncing off of the walls below him. He strained to hear what he was saying to Pop-Pop. Creeping quietly back toward the top of the stairs, he could hear Unc's voice pause and start again, giving Pop-Pop time to catch his breath and say a few words in between. He moved as close as he could to hear Unc's plan for him. Pop-Pop struggled to raise his head to make eye contact with Unc.

With almost a look of defeat, Pop-Pop responded, "You're right, boy. It's only a matter of time before I'll be leaving this place myself."

Benny could hardly believe what he was hearing.

"Pop-Pop is giving up! He always told *me* never to give up,"Benny whispered with intense emphasis.

Benny wasn't interested in hearing any more of the conversation if it meant talk of Pop-Pop dying! When he realized that the conversation was about to end, he turned slowly on his heels to creep back to his room to continue packing.

"How can I leave Pop-Pop to die all alone in a strange place?" Benny whispered as the image of the once energetic Pop-Pop came to mind.

"Surely, Unc won't let that happen," he continued, as he began taking his clothes out of his dresser drawer. "Pop-Pop is the one who had taught me everything I know about baseball. He's the one who encouraged me when I wanted to give up on pitching and on having a normal life," Benny muttered.

A burning sensation rose back up into Benny's chest as he remembered what Pop-Pop said about things not being fair.

"It's not fair for Pop-Pop to be by himself," Benny protested in a louder voice.

But before he could continue his conversation with himself, he glanced down at his faded blue and gold baseball uniform sitting on top of the clothes he had stuffed into his duffle bag. He rubbed his hand over the raised navy blue letters B-U-Z-Z-A-R-D-S suspended above the dingy yellow cotton shirt.

Wiping a tear from the corner of his eye, Benny grabbed his baseball cap from the dresser and adjusted it snugly on his head. He smirked as he announced the nickname, *Cap* that his coaches had given to him.

"Cap the pitcher with the peanut head! I guess they're right, because I can't find a baseball cap to fit my small head nowhere. Now, Cap can't seem to find a place to call home, neither," Benny sighed as he rolled his eyes and ran his fingers over the bill of the cap as if preparing to pitch from the mound.

He reached down into the duffle bag to pull out the baseball glove that Pop-Pop had given him for his 10th birthday, as a memento of Jackie Robinson making his mark in the Major League playing for the Brooklyn Dodgers. The smell of the worn leather caused another pool of tears to form and drip into his glove as he held it against his face. Pop-Pop had helped him break in that glove when it was brand new -- hard and stiff.

"I can still remember Pop-Pop telling me over and over again, '*Take control of the ball, son. You're in control, so let everybody know it!*'" A small smirk forced its way onto Benny's face.

"Yeah, I wish I were *in control* of where I want to live and who I want to live with. I just want to live to be as wise as Pop-Pop one day," Benny sighed again, as he zipped the bag shut. He dragged the heavy khaki bag to the top of the wooden stairs letting it slide down over the edge of each step.

Plunk! Plunk! Plunk!

Finally, he reached the bottom. The loud thud startled Pop-Pop and Unc.

"Ya all packed, son?" Pop-Pop called into the foyer.

"Yep, all packed, Pop-Pop," Benny replied, swallowing hard.

"Well, get on in here and let me take another look at ya before Unc gets ya outta of here," Pop-Pop commanded in his weak raspy voice.

Benny lifted his head and forced a smile to his face just before he entered Pop-Pop's bedroom. Benny stood next to the bed and ran his hand over Pop-Pop's blanket before leaning over to wrap his arms around Pop-Pop for a *good-bye* hug.

But Pop-Pop stuck his right hand out instead.

"We should shake hands like real men, son," Pop-Pop said.

Benny gently clutched his hand around Pop-Pop's cold wrinkled hand.

"Love you, Pop-Pop." Benny said with as much bass as he could bring to his voice. "See you later."

"Love ya, too, son," Pop-Pop whispered, as he released his hand slowly from Benny's.

"Alright, Pop, see you later," Unc said, as he called back toward Pop Pop's bedroom.

As he carried Benny's duffle bag to the car, he let the screen door slam shut behind them, but Benny refused to look back.

As Unc started the car, the young crooner Dion's voice sang softly on the radio:

Drive around the world,

'Cause I'm a wanderer, yeah a wanderer

I roam around-around-around-around-around

'Cause I'm a wanderer, yeah a wanderer

I roam around-around-around-around-around

The words of the song captured just the way Benny felt at this moment and all of his life – like a wanderer roaming around, around, around except he wasn't going around the world, he was going to the other side of the city.

"Cack! Cack! Cack! Cack!"

The music was interrupted by the chickens singing their own off-beat tune. The cackling nearly drowned out the song until Unc reached the corner; then Benny could barely hear them.

"I roam around, and around, and around, and around…"

The drowsy song and sad chicken sendoff caused Benny to wipe away a steady stream of tears as Unc made a right turn away from Pop-Pop's street – the street that he knew as home for his entire life. He craned his neck to look back and get the last glimpse of Pop-Pop's house, but it was no longer in sight.

As he turned to face the windshield, Unc grabbed Benny's shoulder, "Big man, I'm going to take good care of you. I promise."

Benny nodded his head, and whispered back, "I know. That's what Pop-Pop said."

Driving up the street away from Pop-Pop's house toward the U.S. Capitol building, Benny shook his head and whispered under his breath, "I wonder if there's a law against what's happening to me?"

Benny suddenly recalled one day last summer, when a long line of cars drove past Pop-Pop's house. A group of Congressmen visited Southwest D.C. to observe how the Blacks were surviving in one of the poorest neighborhoods of the nation's capital. Their plans included demolishing many of the old houses and businesses in Pop-Pop's neighborhood, and replacing them with new Federal government office buildings and high-rise apartments.

Benny remembered the long line of long black cars that drove past Pop-Pop's house as one of the most exciting days in the neighborhood. Even the reporters who wanted to interview Pop-Pop were surprised to see a house owned by a Black man with electricity and indoor plumbing.

Pop-Pop had worked hard to pay to have electricity and a bathroom inside his house. Most of the other neighbors still had to use kerosene lamps and outhouses. This was only one of the things that made living at Pop-Pop's so special.

But Pop-Pop's lights and working toilet no longer mattered to Benny now, because he was moving to the Northeast section of the city where every house had electricity, plumbing and green grass in the yard. No one

would consider Benny poor anymore.

Chapter 2 - A New Home

It was a long ride to Unc's house. Benny knew that he wouldn't be able to just walk to Pop-Pop's house. Unc turned down one long street after another, left, right, right, left Benny lost track after a while.

The ride was mostly quiet except for the faint sound of songs playing on the car radio, because Unc wasn't a big talker like Pop-Pop. Benny kept replaying Pop-Pop's voice in his head, telling him that he would have a better life with Unc. He began to squirm in his seat each time he thought about Pop-Pop being in the house alone, not knowing when Mama would finally come back.

Finally, Unc made a left turn onto a wide street with one tall oak tree, then a tall pine, and couple more oaks, and three more pines. Benny hadn't seen so many trees on one street before.

Unc pulled over in front of a red brick house with a white picket fence. Though it was getting dark, Benny remembered what Unc's house looked like from the few times he had visited with Mama. There was even a wooden swing on his front porch.

The neighborhood was quiet. No radios played in the windows of the neighbors' houses. There were no children running down the street. And there were no chickens in the front yard to greet him.

Benny gazed up at the dark brown wooden door with the large black painted numbers 6-1-0 down the left side. As Unc opened his door with the army duffle bag in hand, Benny thought back to how green the grass was in

Unc's front yard. It looked almost fake. His yard looked like a picture out of a magazine-- with lots of grass, and no chickens running around.

The smell of Unc's house was different, too. As he entered the foyer, his nose was blanketed by a clean, sterile almost hospital-like smell. The living room was as if decorated for royalty, with an oversized cream-colored sofa and matching chair that sat next to a real piano! Benny remembered Mama mocking Unc's standard speech—"No one is allowed to plop on my furniture, and the piano is reserved for real musicians, not curious children."

"Hang up your jacket, big man," Unc gently instructed Benny just as he was about to sling it onto the living room sofa. It was as if he had read his mind. Pop-Pop didn't make him hang up his clothes; in fact, the only thing hung up in Pop-Pop's house was his *good* navy blue suit that he only wore to church on Easter and Christmas. He always said that he wanted to look his best when he went to the Lord's house.

Other than that blue suit, Pop-Pop just wore his blue jean overalls and dingy white shirt. Anything else he wore was thrown over a chair in his bedroom or wherever he left it.

As Benny finished hanging his jacket, Unc was rattling off yet another set of instructions for him to follow.

"Don't forget to wash those hands before supper. And, you know we go to church on Sunday morning. I'll have to think of a few chores for you to help me with around here, since this is going to be your home for a while," Unc concluded in his military bass tone.

Benny stared toward the kitchen in disbelief for a moment. He couldn't remember being told to wash his hands before digging into a plate of Pop-Pop's crispy fried chicken. And he couldn't understand the purpose of hanging up his jacket when he would be putting it back on the next day.

Benny headed to the spotless bathroom to carry out Unc's second command. It was sparkling white with white painted walls, shiny white sink and toilet.

"Pop-Pop said that Unc was a good man, but he is beginning to be a good pain in the butt," Benny whispered to himself as he glanced into small mirror hanging over the sink. "Things sure are gonna be different here. And I ain't sure that I like all of these new rules," he sighed.

A tightness began to form in Benny's back as he thought about running back to Pop-Pop's house as soon as Unc went to sleep. He knew that wouldn't work. Unc lived too far away from Pop-Pop's. There was no returning to Pop-Pop's house.

"Let me show you where to put your bag," Unc said, interrupting Benny's thoughts of escape.

Unc motioned toward the stairs leading to Benny's bedroom. Benny knew that his room would be immaculate, which caused his back to tighten even more at the thought of having to keep it that way all of the time.

"Sure," he answered, trying to sound enthused.

Unc led Benny down a wide hallway with two bedrooms and another bathroom that had a large white metal bathtub. Benny wanted to peek into Unc's room, but was too anxious to see his own.

"So, what do you think about your new space?" Unc gently asked.

"This is real nice," Benny responded.

He noticed a picture of him that Unc had hanging on his bedroom wall. Unc had framed the team baseball picture that Benny had taken after one of his boy's club games last spring.

"Alright then, I'll let you get unpacked and call you when I have a few vittles together. I know you're starving," Unc said as he turned to walk back down the hallway.

"Okay," Benny replied.

He stared back at his photo and then at the dark wooden furniture that sat perfectly on top of the waxed hardwood floors that made the bedroom smell like freshly cut trees.

"I see Unc made sure I have a desk and chair to do homework," Benny said sarcastically. "This ain't nothin' like my study spot I had at Pop-Pop's kitchen table."

As Benny unpacked his duffle bag he neatly placed the four shirts, three pair of pants, underwear and socks into each of the three cedar-scented dresser drawers. Even though he didn't feel like he was unpacking for the last time, he knew he would not be going back to Pop-Pop's. The thought of never being able to creep downstairs to Pop-Pop's bedroom late at night made his eyes well up again with tears.

"I can't imagine Unc welcoming me to come into his bedroom to sit on his bed and just talk about anything. He just isn't that kind of man. I know he loves me, but it just isn't going to be the same as Pop-Pop's," Benny sighed.

The knot tightened in Benny's back.

"This ain't an overnight stay at Unc's. This is gonna be home for me for a while," Benny whispered.

Chapter 3 - Pop-Pop Flies Away

The burning sunlight hung behind the old red brick building as Benny stared out of the car window.

He couldn't believe that Pop-Pop died almost two weeks after he left to live with Unc. Benny kept replaying his last conversation with Pop-Pop in his mind as he gently rubbed his hands over the stiff wool of his overcoat.

His intestines seemed to be tied into one of those fancy Boy Scout knots that Teddy showed him. Those knots prevented Benny from eating a stack of Unc's melt-in-your-mouth flap jacks that he served oozing with butter and syrup and crispy bacon that left grease streaks on his plate. If the knots weren't there, Benny would have been able to enjoy what he considered the perfect breakfast for a cold February morning.

Unc didn't force him to talk the entire time that they rode through the city. Benny dreaded the thought of seeing Pop-Pop lying inside the church, with a bunch of people staring down at him. Pop-Pop didn't like people getting too close to his face when he was living, and he sure wouldn't like it any more now.

Benny also dreaded seeing Mama who he hadn't seen for a few months when she stopped to get a pair of shoes she left at Pop-Pop's house. Whenever she was questioned about why she left Benny to be raised by Pop-Pop her response was-- "I want to enjoy my youthful years while I can."

"She's so lame," Benny whispered under his breath as Unc drove past a couple of her popular hangouts near the church.

"Come on, son," Unc interjected with his most gentle bass voice as he broke Benny's drifting thoughts. "I know this isn't easy for you, but you have to pay your respects with the rest of the family."

Unc had repeated those very words at least 20 times since the call came from the nursing home that Pop-Pop was found unresponsive lying peacefully in his bed.

"Okay, Unc," Benny replied as he slowly opened the car door.

Benny stared at the black hearse with the Pope Funeral Home sign in the window. This car was a familiar symbol of death in the community.

Unc walked up the concrete stairs of the church ahead of Benny, who hung his head as he watched his feet struggle to lift his nicely polished black wing-tipped shoes onto each step.

Once inside the small white brick building, the two were met by a heavy cloud of men's cologne mixed with a strong scent of women's perfume. The mixture made the air sickeningly sweet as the heavy wooden door closed hard behind Benny. Benny struggled to find a whiff of fresh air as he moved through the bodies crowded at the entrance of the small brick building.

Heads turned as the bass of Unc's voice repeated the phrase "Mornin', how are you?" as he greeted people as they entered the church.

Benny's feet didn't want to move toward the coffin, which lay in the middle of the church. The sea of hand fans slowly motioning back and forth, and the creaking of the wooden pews couldn't distract Benny from the focal point of the room – Pop-Pop's body lying in that shiny black coffin.

"Oh, I'll fly away, old glory, I'll fly away," the choir sang over and over, swaying to the slow, drowsy tempo of the piano as one person after the next walked up to the coffin and looked down at Pop-Pop's lifeless body.

The knots in Benny's stomach would not go away and only grew tighter as the saliva in his mouth and throat dried up. He refused to allow the tears to escape from his eyes as the sniffling and wailing of his aunts and uncles seemed to make his discomfort intensify.

Then his eyes connected with the tear-soaked eyes of Mama, though she didn't seem to recognize him at first. She looked beautiful in a dark blue satin dress. Occasionally, she dabbed her perfectly colored eyelids and neatly powdered cheeks with a red lace handkerchief clutched tightly in her other hand, while holding the hand of one of her man friends with the other.

Sitting next to her on the other side was Uncle Bump. He was taller than Unc with a muscular build. He was a well-known baseball player in the Negro Leagues, but injured himself while on a training mission as an Army paratrooper. Uncle Bump was also known as a ladies' man and was often seen dazzling women with his Hollywood-like smile. He wrapped his long arm around Mama's back to console her.

Benny glanced over at her as he muttered under his breath, "Mama's always gonna make sure she looks good."

As he turned to focus on the black rectangular box that was suspended above a sea of rainbow-colored flowers, Benny didn't have the strength to hold the tears back any longer. He stood over the opening holding Pop-Pop's body. His pale freshly shaven face lay motionless on a silk pillow that held his perfectly round head. The navy blue Sunday suit that hung neatly pressed in his closet was now being worn for the last time.

"Ain't nothing fair in this world, son," kept replaying in Benny's head as he stared at Pop-Pop's chest which seemed to move up and down. The heaviness of the moment created tightness in Benny's chest as he struggled to breathe normally.

Suddenly, the music drowned out the sobs and whispers-- "Just a few more weary days and then, I'll fly away…" the choir sang.

Benny resisted the urge to reach his arms into the casket and lift Pop-Pop up so he could blow a little of his youthful breath into his tightened lips so it could seep inside of his lifeless frame. Instead, he leaned close to Pop-Pop's face and whispered, "I'm a man now, Pop-Pop and I'm gonna make you proud."

Benny turned slowly to sit on the pew in between Uncle Bump and Unc. "This is the worst day of my life," he whispered.

Pop-Pop's gentle soul had truly flown away and there was nothing that Benny could do to bring him back. No one else could possibly understand the pain that he felt inside. The man who loved him more than he loved himself, who pressed through many days of sickness and pain, and spoke the deepest words of wisdom to him was now gone.

"Oh, I'll fly away old glory, I'll fly away," the choir sang in a lower pitch. The man from the funeral home pulled up the thick burgundy colored velvet coffin lining. It now covered Pop-Pop's face, chest, and hands.

In an instant, the singing was overtaken again by the wailing that seemed to shake the tiny church, followed by a rolling wave of screams and deep sobs. The high-pitch sobbing yanked the knots loose in Benny's stomach as he released the loudest cry he had ever heard come out of his own mouth. Lena reached past Uncle Bump to grab his hand, but he ignored her attempt to comfort him. In fact, her hand felt icy cold.

At that moment, he didn't care if anybody heard him. He was losing his Pop-Pop forever. He would never hear his gentle voice, eat crispy fried chicken, lie beside him on his bed during a thunderstorm, or help him feed the crazy chickens early in the morning.

His days with Pop-Pop had come to an end and he would have to wait until his own time came to *fly* away before he would see him again.

Chapter 4 - New Cats in a New Neighborhood

Almost 4 months had passed since Pop-Pop's funeral. Benny was beginning to get used to following Unc's weekly schedule and list of chores. Unc organized Benny's days so tightly so he wouldn't have time to get into any trouble. He was also determined to help Benny understand the importance of getting a good education.

Unc's weekly schedule required Benny to set aside time for learning a new list of vocabulary words, going to church, working on his pitching game, cleaning his room, taking out the trash, and washing the dishes.

Of all of Unc's rules, the hardest ones for Benny to follow were the rules that he had to ask permission to go outside, and he had to come in the house by supper time. For a teenage boy who wasn't used to living under such strict conditions, these were rules that continued to get Benny into trouble. But he didn't want to lose the privilege that Unc promised to allow Teddy to come and visit him once a month.

Pop-Pop didn't care how long Benny hung outside with his friends just as long as he got to school on time every day. On any Friday or Saturday night, Benny could be found outside until the wee hours of the morning. Pop-Pop knew he could be found sitting on the stoop of a neighbor's house playing cards or just listening to music.

Benny woke up excited to explore the neighborhood. After getting dressed he called into Unc's bedroom to ask his permission to walk to the playground.

"Unc, is it okay if I walk down to the playground for a while?" he asked with a little hesitation in his voice.

"Okay," Unc responded, "But don't go wondering off too far.

"I won't," Benny responded with a smirk.

He grabbed his baseball cap and walked up the street toward the neighborhood playground where a group of boys were standing around laughing and talking with each other. He had heard the faint laughter from his bedroom window a few minutes earlier.

"This sure isn't like Southwest. It's *too* quiet 'round here," he muttered as he slowly walked toward them. "I sure hope these *cats* are cool," he whispered to himself as he approached the group. "They look a little uppity, but

I guess I'll have to check 'em out for myself," Benny encouraged himself as he built up his confidence.

The conversation got louder as Benny continued to drag his feet over the dirt path leading right up to where the boys were standing.

"Hey, how y'all doin'?" Benny paused. "My name's Benny," he said slowly, followed by a half grin as if they were supposed to recognize him.

The boys stared at him for a moment without responding, but Benny continued with his introduction.

"I'm from Half Street, Southwest, but I'm staying around here with my uncle for a little while," he ran his hand across B-U-Z-ZA-R-D-S, the raised letters on his shirt. Benny followed by an extension of his hand for a clasped-finger handshake.

"Buzzards, huh?" a husky voice called out, acknowledging the team name on his baseball jersey.

"My name is Pudge."

The voice didn't quite match the short chubby body that stood in front of him as a stubby hand extended toward Benny's hand.

"Yeah," Benny slowly responded. "I pitched for them for a li'l bit in the Walter Johnson League for the past four years. Which league do you dudes play for?" Benny asked as he tried to remain smug and not make a big deal of his star pitching days with his old team.

"All the cats around here play for Number 11 Boys Club," another boy responded. "They call me Shoo-Shoo, dude, 'cause I can't stand thost gnats flying near my handsome face!"

As he walked closer to Benny, the tallest of the group blurted out, "I'm Kirby." Suddenly he looked into Benny's face and said, "Hey, I remember you, man!"

Kirby's eyes widened as if he'd seen a ghost.

"Yeah, y'all—remember that cat who struck all of us out?" he recalled. "We played this dude last year in the playoffs and they spanked us bad!"

"Oh yea," Pudge finally recalled. "You did show some skills in that game, man."

"So, what brings you to *this* side of town?" Kirby chimed in.

"I'm staying with my uncle down the street for a while until my mom gets settled into her new place," Benny responded, knowing that he had to make them think that his life was just as normal as theirs.

"You stayin' with big man in 610, Principal Turner?" a high-pitched voice shrieked, this time from the most muscular boy in the group. His voice almost made Benny chuckle from the thought of a soft girlie tone coming from his big body.

"I'm Patch. Sorta the biggest dude out here," Patch jokingly added allowing Benny to finally release his pinned up laughter.

"I live about two doors down from Mr. Turner," Patch added.

"Yea, things are copasetic, man," Benny responded. "I'm adjusting to my uncle's military schedule. He's cool and all, but I miss my *cats* in Southwest. Dig?" Benny made sure that he spoke with the deepest tone he could eke out to make his coolest first impression.

"So, you wanna play ball with us tomorrow?" Patch asked staring Benny down as a friendly challenge.

"Sure. My uncle and I are actually going to pick up one of my cats tonight from 'round the way so he can hang out with me this weekend," Benny responded as he leaned against the fence with a little more ease.

"Cool. Come back up to the 'ground tomorrow around 2:00, and we'll see what y'all got," Pudge said as he extended his hand to Benny for a farewell handshake.

Benny headed back to Unc's house grinning from ear to ear. But suddenly his grin disappeared and a serious look appeared on his face.

"Teddy can't play no ball with these guys. They'll run circles around him. We're gonna get burned!" Benny muttered to himself.

Chapter 5 – A Visit to Old Stomping Ground

"Benny, you ready to head downtown?" Unc shouted up the stairs.

"I sure am. Been ready to go see my cats," Benny caught himself in mid-sentence when he noticed the frown on Unc's face.

"Cats? Would you happen to be referring to your friends?" Unc promptly corrected.

"Of course, I'm just excited to go back to my old neighborhood," Benny responded as he rubbed his hands together in anticipation.

"Alright, then let's get going," Unc said.

The drive to Southwest seemed to take forever. Benny concluded that either Unc was driving extra slow, or the streets had gotten extra-long. It had been a while since he had seen his old friends and his old house, Pop-Pop's house.

Finally, the last three turns -- left, right, and left – but something wasn't quite the same.

"Hey, where's Normandy's corner store?" Benny asked Unc.

"Gone," Unc responded abruptly.

"Gone?" Benny responded in disbelief. His eyes widened like an owl.

"Yeah, just like all of the houses and stores that used to be on P Street and First Street. They have decided to *revitalize* Southwest," Unc explained in his formal principal voice.

"It seems the government decided it was time to make Southwest look more like a city worthy to be called the nation's capital instead of a big back yard full of run-down buildings with poor people occupying them."

"Revitalize? Run down? You mean they tore down our neighborhood!" Benny exclaimed. "I bet those White men were planning to do this all along! They came down here and took pictures! Laughed and made like they were coming to help us. They talked about how they were going to fix things up-- make things better! Yeah, right!" Benny protested loudly.

Before he could continue, Unc interjected and pointed toward Teddy sitting on the front stoop of his house with his large navy blue duffle bag beside him.

"There's your buddy, all ready to go," Unc chuckled.

"That's Teddy. Always ready. That boy ain't -- I mean is *never* late!" Benny blurted out as a smile stretched across his face.

"Benny!"

Teddy ran to the car window and gave Benny one of their handshake's through the window before Unc could finish parking the car.

"Hey, man, you'd better let Unc stop the car before you get your feet run over!" Benny laughed as Teddy flung open the door to give him a bear hug.

"Man, you've gotten a little taller since I saw you at Pop-Pop's Uh . . .," Benny paused as he quickly changed the subject.

Benny tried to make Teddy feel good about being short for his age. Teddy was almost the same size as he was in the fourth grade. Wearing his favorite plaid buttoned shirt neatly tucked into his pants, Teddy resembled a Black version of Howdy Doody, one of the well-known freckled-face cartoon characters, as he displayed all of his bucked teeth.

"Let me go and speak to your folks, Teddy," Unc announced as he walked up to the front door to greet Mr. Ford.

"Man, I sure have missed you," Teddy replied.

"It seems like everybody has moved away. Have you seen what they're doing to our street?" Teddy asked.

Pointing at the vacant lots where houses once stood, Teddy began to call out the names of their friends whose families were forced to move.

"Remember, Mikey?" Teddy pointed to one pile of rumble where Mikey's house once stood.

"Yeah, Benny responded, raising one eyebrow.

"Gone!" Teddy shouted, with a swift clap of his hands.

"And Lil' Frank?" Teddy pointed toward another pile of bricks and broken wood planks scattered around on yet another vacant lot in the opposite direction of the street.

"Uh-huh", Benny shook his head slowly.

"Gone, too!" Teddy clapped his hands again in an upward direction as if the family had taken off in an airplane.

"And the Chapmans?" Teddy continued his series of short questions and answers.

"What? This is crazy!" Benny shouted, with both fists clenched as if preparing to go after the culprits who destroyed his neighborhood.

"You know my folks are planning to move up there near your Unc's house as soon as my dad starts his new government job next month," Teddy continued. "And that means I won't be going to Armstrong next year. I'll be going to Cardozo with you!" Teddy said with excitement. So, how has it been living with your uncle?" he glanced at Benny's distracted face.

Armstrong was one of the four high schools for Black students in D.C. with a focus on vocational education. Phelps was the other, while Paul Lawrence Dunbar prepared students for college. Cardozo was designed to help students get Federal government office jobs.

Benny tried to act excited about Teddy moving closer to Unc's house. But as he looked at the evidence of destruction that surrounded him he knew that his old neighborhood was quickly disappearing. Everything he remembered as a boy was being erased forever.

"So, how bad is it living with your uncle," Teddy asked again trying to change Benny's focus from the devastation around him.

Benny struggled to continue his conversation with Teddy as he stared at all of the piles of rubble that lined the street that he once walked to school.

"Naw, it hasn't been too bad, but he's been gettin' a little crazy with the rules and all," Benny stated, "especially, making me ask permission to go outside! I mean, come on, I'm going to be in high school this year!" Benny exclaimed raising both arms in the air.

Both boys chuckled aloud.

"Hey, I met some pretty cool cats up the street on the playground near my uncle's house. They're looking for us to play ball with them tomorrow," Benny announced waiting to get a reaction from Teddy.

"Cool!" Teddy responded.

"You mean, you're gonna play?" Benny asked in amazement.

"Yeah, man. I've been sharpening up on my game since you left," Teddy swung an imaginary bat. "I'm ready to play, no joke," Teddy yelled enthusiastically.

"I don't believe it," Benny looked wide-eyed at Teddy as if looking at a stranger. You never wanted to play ball with us before. You were always the one keeping score! What changed your mind?" Benny asked with a puzzled look.

"Well, when you left, I realized that I had to figure out a way to fit in with the other guys. No one was going to play chess with me like you. So, I asked my dad to teach me the game, just like your Pop-Pop did for you," Teddy stopped talking when he noticed Benny's blank stare.

"Man, I sure do miss Pop-Pop," Benny said as he turned toward the direction of his old street. "I know they're gonna knock his house down next."

Teddy put his hand on Benny's shoulder, "It's already gone, man."

Benny ran to the corner of the street and looked toward the concrete steps that led up to an empty lot where Pop-Pop's house used to be.

"No way! How can they do this?" Benny squatted with his hands resting on his thighs. "They must have been just waiting for Pop-Pop to die!"

He never imagined that Pop-Pop's house would become one of the houses to be torn down. What once was his place of comfort was now a pile of dirt, rocks and broken wood that was once used to be the fence to keep the chickens in the yard. There weren't any chickens running around in the yard. Uncle Bump gave the chickens to Normandy's to sell as fried chicken dinners and sandwiches. There was nothing special about having electricity anymore, because a new office building would now sit in the spot that Benny used to call home.

Teddy ran mid-way behind him, but stopped to give him a moment to take it all in. He waited for Benny to walk slowly back toward him, dragging his feet as if defeated by an invisible giant.

"Come on," Teddy, he said with a sigh. "Let's get ready to go," Benny hung his head and walked toward Unc's car in silence.

Chapter 6 – A Dangerous Adventure

Benny and Teddy stayed up all night talking about old times after filling up on peanut butter and jelly sandwiches and milk. Unc sat in the living room reading one of his many books and seemingly unbothered by the loud talking between the boys.

"So, are you *really* ready to play these cats tomorrow? Benny asked sarcastically.

"Yeah, I'm ready," Teddy insisted, "I'm tellin' you, Benny, I can actually hit the ball now and I can even make it to first base!" Teddy boasted hitting his fist against his chest. He motioned as if swinging a bat and running across Unc's hardwood floors.

"Alright fellas, take that running outside," Unc yelled toward the stairs.

Benny motioned to Teddy to quiet down. "See what I mean, Unc has a lot of rules, man, a lot of rules," Benny flopped backward onto his bed as if falling into a swimming pool.

"But I guess I should be glad that I've got a place to call home," he continued.

Teddy looked compassionately at his best friend's face and shook his head in agreement.

"Well, you know we'll practically be neighbors again soon, and I'll be calling this nice quiet neighborhood, home, too," Teddy reassured Benny.

Benny tried to work up a chuckle. "Man, you are so blessed to have a mom and dad to live with."

"*Blessed*?" Teddy repeated, "You gone religious on me now?"

"Naw, I just understand that you have something that I don't have and probably never will," Benny sighed as he picked up his baseball glove and pounded his fist into the pocket of the glove.

"It's like pitching a game blindfolded. Not knowing where the ball is going once it's released from my hand; with no direction just flying in the air. That's how I feel sometimes-- like I'm in an eternally pitch black room trying to feel my way out," Benny stated in his most mature voice.

"Wow, man, that's deep," Teddy whispered.

"Well, that's enough of that moping stuff, let's rest up for the game tomorrow," Benny slapped Teddy on the back of his head.

"Alright, man, you know I'm gonna get you back," Teddy warned pointing at Benny. "You'd better keep one eye open tonight!"

The birds chirping outside of Benny's bedroom window were his natural wake-up call. The sweltering D.C. heat seeping through the window screens of his bedroom window was a reminder that summertime had arrived.

"Teddy, time to rise and shine," Benny leaned over and yelled into Teddy's ear.

Teddy jumped up from his pallet on the floor.

"Huh? What?"

"Come on, man, we need to get some grub and get to the field to practice before we take on those slick cats today," Benny's urging mimicked Unc's commands.

"It won't take me long to get myself together. I bet I'll even beat you downstairs," Teddy challenged.

Benny resisted the temptation to race him to the staircase fearing that Unc would bark out another reprimand about running in the house. After making their way to the kitchen, Benny noticed a note that Unc had left for him on the kitchen table.

Benny,

I've gone to a meeting at the church. Make sure you and Teddy eat a bowl of cereal before you go outside, and don't forget to lock the door. I expect to see you and Teddy in the neighborhood when I return this afternoon.

Unc

"Shucks, we can skip this breakfast stuff and walk to the corner store and get a couple of Rock Creek grape sodas," Benny shouted.

Teddy wasn't sure how to respond, but soon chimed in hesitantly.

"Yeah, let's get a couple of sodas and a bag of Bon-Ton potato chips, too!" Teddy exclaimed.

The two hurried to get washed up and dressed, anxious to take advantage of the few hours of freedom before Unc returned.

As Benny and Teddy began walking toward the playground, Benny stopped suddenly and turned toward Teddy.

"Hey, man we should scrap this game and take a little trip across the bridge to check out that White team that we saw riding on that nice bus down M Street last year," Benny recalled.

Benny rubbed his hand over the bill of his baseball cap in excitement. He still wasn't convinced that Teddy was ready to play ball against his new neighbors.

"That's a good idea, we can go over there and spy them out," Teddy responded with excitement, "I'm ready to finally do something I'm *not* supposed to do."

Teddy rubbed his hands together and flashed Benny a devilish grin. He un-tucked his shirt from his pants and tried to imitate Benny's slow stride down the street.

Just then, Benny spotted Shoo-Shoo, Kirby, Patch, Pudge walking toward the playground.

"Hey, wait up," Benny yelled. Unc would have definitely frowned upon him yelling down the street and described his actions as uncouth. Teddy kept pace with Benny's fast stride that quickly advanced to a slow jog as he clutched his baseball glove under his arm.

"What's up, Benny?" Pudge said. "You ready for a rematch?"

"Sure, man, but first I want you to meet one of my best friends from my old neighborhood. This is my ace, Teddy," Benny said.

Benny slapped Teddy on the back while pushing him closer to the other boys.

"Hey, how ya doing? I'm Kirby?"

"And I'm Pudge," the two boys almost said in unison.

"How ya doing, little man? I'm Shoo-Shoo" Shoo-Shoo belted out while extending his hand to test Teddy's ability to respond appropriately with a hand grip.

Patch gave Teddy a quick, "Hey," as he stared at Teddy's outfit.

"I'm good," Teddy responded as he extended his hand to connect with Shoo-Shoo's.

"Hey, fellas, I have an idea and I wanna know if you're game." Benny perked up in anticipation of going outside of Unc's boundaries.

"What you tryin' to do, man?" Kirby asked with curiosity.

"Well, I figure Teddy is visiting this weekend and we have a whole day to hang out without my uncle breathing down our necks. So, I'm thinking we can take a little trip across the bridge to check out those White cats in Barry Farms."

Benny could barely get the sentence out of his mouth, before Patch interjected--

"Man, you must be crazy! Have you ever been in the Farms? Do you know they have some crazy Sons of B's over there! I mean, they can play some ball 'cause they got all of that fancy equipment and stuff, but they don't take to us Black bruthas intruding on their territory," Patch stated firmly.

Kirby chimed in, "Ah, come on Patch, you ain't never been to the Farms. All you know is what you heard your brother making up in his crazy mind. I say let's do it, I've always wanted to see what their side of town looks like. I heard you can see their green playing field as soon as you cross the bridge," Kirby continued.

Pudge snickered and shook his head, "Yeah, I ain't got nothing else to do."

"Alright, Shoo-Shoo, are you in or what?" Benny asked impatiently as he began walking backward down the street leading to the South Capitol Street bridge.

"Sure, just what I wanted to do today-- go watch a bunch of Crackers play ball on their expensive baseball field," Shoo-Shoo replied rolling his eyes in his head.

"Let's get going then," Benny put his hand into his glove and punched his fist into the pocket, which was his trade mark before facing an opponent on the mound.

As they walked past Unc's yard, Benny tossed his baseball glove onto the porch so it landed under the swing. Teddy tried to strike up conversation with Pudge as they walked next to each other down the street.

"So, how'd you do the last reporting period of school?" Teddy said to Pudge as he struggled to keep up with his slightly faster stride.

"Reporting period? Man, I barely made it out of junior high school! Heck, I was just glad to see all them D's on my report card!" Pudge replied as he belted out a laugh.

"Ooooo-kay," Teddy responded with a look of bewilderment.

Pretty soon, Teddy found himself catching up to keep pace with Benny, who was outpacing everyone else.

"We've gotta get over here and back before Unc gets back home," Benny whispered to Teddy. "Now if you don't want to do this, we can always say that we forgot to do some chores at the Unc's house and turn back."

"Naw, man, this is the most fun I've had in a long time, Teddy insisted. "Besides, I've got to prove to these cats that I can hang since I'm gonna be moving up here soon."

"Alright, but stay close to me once we get over to the other side," Benny whispered in a fatherly tone.

"Man, this is a hike," Pudge complained. "This heat is draining me. I bet I've lost a good 10 pounds already."

"I know, man, and I can't afford to lose any weight," Kirby replied wiping sweat as it dripped from his forehead.

"Don't know why y'all complaining," Patch said as he wiped sweat from his face, "Remember, y'all wanted to walk over here," he continued rolling his eyes in disgust.

The boys trek across the bridge soon ended at a complete stop as they all suddenly stopped to take in the view ahead of them. They were about to enter Southeast.

"Have you ever seen so much green grass before in all your life?" Benny exclaimed.

Southeast was the all-White section of D.C. where the baseball fields were considered the best playing fields in the city. The grass was freshly cut and the baseball diamond was perfectly shaped. The boys' club teams wore uniforms and used equipment that resembled a minor league baseball team.

"Hey, there's the Spartan field over there," Teddy yelled out as he trotted toward the open gate.

"Fool, don't you know that we can't just walk through the front gate of their field. We ain't exactly welcome on this side of town --remember?" Kirby's voice quivered as he cautioned Teddy.

"We have to go around and look through the fence from the back field where no one will see us," Patch said pointing toward an opening.

The boys made their way to the wooded area and positioned themselves in the brush lining the back fence. They watched as the Spartans' crisp white uniforms with black lettering began to gather on the field. The names of each player could be seen boldly stitched across their back as they took a lap around the bases. The players ran with the precision of Marines preparing for a military drill at the Marine Barracks.

The look on each player's face was serious. There was no laughing and fooling around on the field. The coach barked out instructions and they all quickly responded.

"Dag, they don't look like they're enjoying what they're doing at all," Benny noted as he watched the robotic-like movements that the team made.

"Our team would have been cutting up with a few jokes and crackin' up laughing by now," Pudge chimed in.

"Hey! What you boys doing over here?" A raspy voice called from behind them.

Startled, Benny and his friends turned toward the voice in almost the same precision as the team was running their lap.

"Uh, we're just checking out the team practice," Benny replied trying to maintain a calm tone.

"Checking out *our* Spartans, huh?" another chunky

White boy wearing a dirty white t-shirt and jeans with a hole in the knee said as he frowned at Benny's explanation.

"I think these boys are lying", a tall red-face boy with fire red hair shouted. "In fact, I think you're over here trying to steal our team's equipment!"

"Man, you need to chill with that!" Kirby responded angrily. "Ain't nobody trying to steal nobody's equipment!"

As the exchange continued between Kirby and the gang of White teens, Benny glanced around the group of boys to determine their best route of escape. Just then, the red-face boy began to walk closer toward Pudge as if to take a swing.

"Break!" Benny yelled, which was well understood signal to run as fast as you could in whatever direction you could.

Shoo-Shoo turned to follow right behind Benny and Kirby with Pudge not far behind. Benny turned slightly to encourage Teddy to stretch his short legs.

"Come on Teddy long strides, man," Benny shouted.

But Teddy was too afraid and hesitated to respond at Benny's first signal. He soon found himself trailing far behind the other boys. He tripped over a tree stump and fell face forward to the ground.

"Benny, help!" Teddy yelled as he struggled to get up, but the gang just pushed his small body back down to the ground.

Benny stopped suddenly as Patch, Pudge and Kirby ran passed him.

"Teddy!" Benny yelled.

His heart was pounding fast as he ran back toward Teddy. His feet swished through the tall blades of grass and his arms cut through the hot summer air as he pressed to get across the field. Teddy looked like a soccer ball being kicked across the ground.

"Get off of him!" Benny yelled.

His attempt to force the group to come after him failed as the swinging and kicking motions never paused, but continued to focus on the small object now lying limp on the ground.

Pudge, Shoo-Shoo, Patch, and Kirby turned to run behind Benny. All four boys prepared for the worst as they watched the relentless quick kicks, stomps and punches that made it hard to see Teddy's blue plaid shirt.

As Benny drew closer, the group began to run away laughing and taunting the boys for crossing the bridge and trespassing into their neighborhood. Their chants of victory disappeared with them as they ran deep into the wooded area at the other end of the field like a pack of wild wolves.

Red splotches covered the ground in a trail leading to Teddy's blood soaked shirt. His small motionless body looked like a deflated ball surrounded by a growing watery red circle on the ground.

Benny slid on his knees across the soft grass beside Teddy; he rolled his limp body over toward him.

"Teddy! Teddy, you alright?" Benny cried out.

Tears streaming down his face mixed with the sweat that was pouring down his neck.

Benny touched Teddy's neck to feel for a pulse, but Teddy did not respond. His eyes were wide open as if staring at the hazy sky, but his chest was not moving up and down. There was no air coming out of his nose or mouth. The back of his head was cut open like a melon.

"I told him to stay close. I told him," Benny whispered between heavy breaths, "God help us."

Looking up into the sun beaming down on his face, Benny could hear Pop-Pop's voice softly telling him, "Ya make choices in life that aren't always the best, but ya have to live with the consequences nonetheless."

The words cut through Benny's heart, as he knew the choice he made today was one of the worst choices he had ever made in his life. Soon, Pudge, Shoo-Shoo, Patch and Kirby were standing over Benny in silence as they watched him gently lift Teddy's bloodied head close to his chest. Benny rubbed his thin hand across Teddy's forehead and sobbed violently.

I'm so sorry, Teddy. It's my fault. I shouldn't have left you, man. I'm sorry!" Benny cried out.

A couple of the baseball coaches from the Spartan's team ran toward the boys.

"What happened here? Is this boy okay?" The taller of the two men asked.

"Those crazy White bastards beat up my best friend for no good reason," Benny shouted." They just kicked him and stomped him 'til he wasn't breathing no more!" He shouted as he stared into Teddy's motionless eyes.

"This boy has lost a lot of blood. He needs to go to the hospital right away," the other man replied, "We need to call an ambulance."

The other man jogged back toward the baseball field as the taller man watched Benny cradle Teddy's body in his arms like a baby.

"We didn't come over here to cause no trouble, sir," Pudge chimed in still trying to catch his breath.

"Yeah, we only wanted to see how your boys practiced. That's all we wanted to do," Kirby added as he began to sob.

"And those boys came after us like mad men accusing us of trying to steal your team's equipment. Teddy just couldn't get away," Patch chimed in wiping his eyes.

"Well, you know you boys took a big risk coming over here. Where do you live?" he asked.

"We live by Cardozo High School in Northeast," Benny eked out just above a whisper.

"Why in the world would you come all the way over here?" the man asked. He was wearing a white t-shirt with the word *Coach* printed on the left side of his chest. He rubbed his head and he looked puzzled by their response.

"We only wanted to watch your boys practice. We didn't come over here trying to start no trouble," Kirby began to sob.

"Yeah, but trouble was waiting for you and now it looks like your friend paid the price for *your* curiosity," the coach responded coldly.

The coach knelt down on one knee to get closer to Teddy's lifeless body and touched his bloody forehead. He shook his head as he inhaled and then exhaled deeply as if wishing that Teddy could do the same on his own.

He turned to the boys and said, "You know your friend is barely clinging to life, and the guys that did this to your friend are gonna stay low for a few days. Even if anyone knows about what they've done, they aren't gonna turn them over to the law. You boys gotta know that we live in a different world over here and life ain't always fair."

Those words pierced Benny in the heart as he heard Pop Pop's voice echo the same words, "Life ain't fair."

The other coach yelled across the field, "The ambulance is coming, but don't know if they'll take him." He was referring to the closest hospital, Cafritz Hospital that was known for turning away Black patients. However, none of the boys responded.

Benny closed his eyes and rocked Teddy's body slowly.

"Teddy, please breathe. Please breathe," Benny whispered over and over again as the other boys helplessly looked on.

———————————

"Hello, anybody home?" Unc called upstairs to Benny and Teddy, expecting to have seen them outside on the playground when he drove up the street.

Benny heard Unc call him, but didn't answer. He sank deep into his bed with his head buried under his pillow.

"Oh God, how am I going to tell Unc about what we did *today*, Benny moaned rubbing his hand over his chest as if consoling himself. "He probably thinks we spent the day hanging around in the neighborhood. I know he's going to be disappointed if he finds out from Mr. Ford what happened before I tell him," Benny mumbled to himself.

"Benny? Teddy? You boys up there?" Unc called up the stairs in an even louder tone.

Unc walked up the stairs double time clutching Benny's baseball glove under his arm. His hard bottom shoes pounded against each wooden step and sounded like an army approaching Benny's bedroom.

"Yes, I'm in here," Benny responded quietly, his voice crackling.

The reality of his best friend's death continued to replay in his head.

Unc slowly opened the door to find Benny lying flat across his bed, still wearing his shoes and baseball cap. Both were a sign to Unc that something was wrong.

"Hey son, where's Teddy?" Unc asked as he laid Benny's glove on his desk.

Unc looked at Benny's body slowly turn toward him. His face was wet with fresh tears that seemed to form parallel lines to the dried zigzag lines that stretched from underneath his eyes to his chin.

"What in the world happened between you and Teddy? Did something happen with those boys down the street?" Unc asked in a panic.

Unc's voice had escalated to an alarmed tone as he looked around Benny's room to see Teddy's duffle bag still lying in the corner.

"Did Teddy's father come and get him?" Unc continued to question Benny, but there was only silence as Benny stared with horror into Unc's eyes.

"I- I made a big mistake, today, Unc," Benny struggled to get the words to come out. "Me and Teddy were supposed to play ball with the dudes down the street, but when I realized you would be gone most of the day, I suggested that we go over the bridge and watch the White team practice instead."

"Wait a minute! Are you telling me that you went across the bridge to *Barry Farms* today?" Unc asked.

The wrinkles in his forehead deepened as he thought about what could happen to any Black person found on the other side of town uninvited.

"Yes, sir," Benny mumbled. "That's exactly what we did. Teddy said he wanted to go, but I knew it was a bad idea once we started walking toward the bridge. I told him that we could make up a story to the guys and turn back, but he didn't want to," Benny said as he wiped tears from his eyes.

Benny could sense the disappointment in Unc's voice.

"So what exactly happened?" Unc asked as his voice intensified.

He had now taken two more steps closer to Benny's bed as if to make sure he could hear Benny's explanation clearly.

"Well, once we got to the other side, we spotted a place in the woods behind their field where we could watch the White team practice without being noticed. We were just so amazed by their nice uniforms and all of the green grass they had on their baseball field.

Just as they started running the bases, a group of crazy White boys came up behind us talking trash and accusing us of trying to steal the team's equipment," Benny continued trying to avoid eye contact with Unc.

Benny paused to catch his breath as he described how quickly the events happened, but Unc motioned with his hands insisting that he continue. His face wrinkled up even more than before as he now stood over Benny with his lips parted to reveal the large gap between his two front teeth that made he and Lena look like twins.

"Well, we told them we only came to watch their team practice and even Kirby told them we didn't want any trouble, but they ignored everything we said." Benny's voice cracked as he was now sitting up with his feet firmly planted on the side of his bed.

"They kicked and beat Teddy so bad, Unc, as if he weren't even human. I've never seen evil and hatred like that before, and I never want to ever again!" Benny's voice reduced to a whisper as he hung his head in disbelief.

"So where is Teddy now?" Unc anxiously asked with a puzzled look on his face.

"He's dead, Unc," Benny whispered.

"Dead?" Unc yelled.

Benny continued, "One of the White coaches called an ambulance, and rode with him to Cafritz Hospital. He told us we needed to get home before those guys decided to come back and cause more trouble. So when the ambulance came, we ran as fast as we could back across the bridge! I didn't want to leave Teddy! I feel terrible!" Benny shouted as he jumped up to look out of the window.

"Benny, do you realize how bad this is? Teddy is *dead*, because you demonstrated poor judgment, son. Very poor judgment," Unc said sternly.

"Look at me son. This is not good," Unc emphasized as he looked into Benny's eyes and shook his head in disappointment.

"Because of your rebellion, you cost your best friend his life," Unc continued. "I can't imagine how Mr. and Mrs. Ford must be feeling right now!"

"I know! I know!" Benny shouted as he looked back out of the window, and pounded his hand on top of his glove lying on the desk.

"We need to drive over to Teddy's parents' house right now so you can tell them exactly what happened. They need to know that he's *not* alright, if the hospital hasn't already reached them! I know they are going to be upset to learn that not only did I neglect to take care of their son, but his best friend didn't protect him either," Unc's voice boomed against the bedroom walls.

Benny looked at Unc with tears in his eyes. An expression he was not used to seeing from such a strong man.

As Unc left Benny's room to walk back down the stairs, he called back tell Benny to grab Teddy's bag. Benny immediately responded as he trailed behind. In that moment, he whispered to himself, I guess Pop-Pop was right when he said, '*Ain't nothing fair in this world.*' I should have been the one to die today, not Teddy!"

A steady stream of tears ran down Benny's face and blurred his vison as he blindly walked down the stairs.

Chapter 7 - Lonely Summer – 1952

Benny walked close to Unc as they passed by small groups of people gathered on the sidewalk outside of Friendship Baptist Church. It seemed like the same group of people that Benny recognized from Pop-Pop's funeral just a few months ago, except there seemed to be younger faces mixed into the crowd.

The line of people waiting to enter the tiny white building stretched near the entrance where Normandy's once stood nearly two blocks away. The sun seemed to have picked Benny's scalp to rest its rays like a laser beam.

Benny couldn't help but think that it was God's way of punishing him for disobeying Unc or maybe it was a reminder to Benny that he was the cause of Teddy's death.

Unc interrupted Benny's train of thought as he asked, "Are you alright, son?"

Wiping the annoying drips of tears that kept streaming down his cheeks Benny whispered, "Yes, sir."

Just then, a coffee brown shiny face peered out from the wooden doors of the church yelling out to Unc and Benny.

"Mr. Turner, you and Benny can come on in, a soft voice called."

"Come on, son. But that child ought to know that you do not yell down the street. It's awfully disrespectful to the family," Unc murmured to Benny.

The girl motioned to them to follow her direction. As they reached the front steps, Unc recognized the young girl's face as one of his former elementary school students, Hattie Bea Garrison.

"How y'all doing?" Hattie asked in a quieter tone.

"Fine, and you young lady?" Unc responded giving her a half smile.

Benny did not respond to the bright-eyed girl who he had once had a crush on in elementary school. His eyes were burning from the tears that had flowed from his eyes the night before. The familiar sickening scent of men's cologne and women's perfume mixed together and thickened the air in the church. He almost had to gasp for air as the heat caused his tie to squeeze his neck.

"I'll fly away, fly away, old glory. I'll fly away…" the choir sang the same familiar sad song.

Benny's stomach twisted into tight knots as the pair walked slowly down the middle aisle and passed by each row of pews. Benny noticed the seated bodies reposition and turn toward them causing the old wood to creak. Benny felt like a prisoner going before a firing squad as he looked up occasionally and met the eyes of his former classmates sobbing and shaking their heads.

Soon they reached the pew where Mr. and Mrs. Ford sat staring at the small dark brown coffin that held Teddy's body. It was covered with bright red roses and large bouquets of flowers sitting on metal stands on both sides of the closed shiny container. Unc had already explained to Benny that Teddy's skull was crushed from the beating and his parents did not want the casket to be open during the funeral.

Benny could hardly contain himself as he knelt in front of the casket, laying his shaking hand on the side of the cold casket. The tears poured down his face as Unc put his hand on his shoulder. The scene caused the crowd of people sitting in the pews to sob loudly.

"It's alright, son. Teddy is in a much better place now," Unc whispered in his low bass voice, "He's going to keep Pop-Pop company until you get there."

"But I'm gonna miss him, Unc. He was too young to die," Benny whispered as Unc helped him back to his feet.

Mr. Ford joined the two as they turned to walk back to the sit down. He reached past Unc to pull Benny close to him.

"Son, this wasn't your fault and I don't want you beating yourself up about it. Teddy's going to be okay now. He's gonna be okay," Mr. Ford whispered into Benny's ear.

As he tightly hugged Benny, he caused Benny to sob even louder.

The hot and hazy days of summer seemed to just come and go. Benny lost his desire to hang out with his new friends. Unc was concerned that Benny was not eating and had lost a lot of weight from his thin body. Unc knocked on the bedroom door that remained closed more than it was open.

"Benny, can I come in?" Unc's voice bounced off of the hallway walls.

"Come on in," Benny responded.

He was lying on his back staring at the ceiling with his baseball glove on his right hand.

"Son, why don't you go on outside and play ball with your friends? You know you need to practice your spiral pitch," Unc encouraged. "You're going to turn into a sack of bones, lying in this room every day. Pretty soon you'll be starting high school!"

Unc's attempt to make Benny smile failed. Unc sat on the corner of the bed and laid his large hand on Benny's thigh.

"You know I will be taking a trip to Europe in a few weeks as part of that principal exchange program I told you about. So I've been talking to your Uncle Bump about you staying with him for a while until I get back," Unc said.

Benny sprang up in the bed as if pricked with a pin.

"Live with Uncle Bump?" Benny yelled out in amazement.

"Yes, I think it may be good for both of you. But it will only be for eight months," Unc emphasized.

"No, I like that idea, Unc," Benny responded, hitting his hand into the pocket of his glove. "I'd love to live with Uncle Bump."

Benny knew that he would have more freedom at Uncle Bump's house. Uncle Bump had earned his nickname after "bumping off" his opponents as a well-known baseball and softball player in D.C.

Unc deepened his voice as he looked into Benny's eyes, "Now remember, this won't be a permanent living arrangement. Uncle Bump will have to slow down a bit to make sure you're getting your books and staying . . ."

"Out of trouble," Benny completed Unc's sentence.

But this time Unc didn't mind the interruption. Benny had already learned that lesson the hard way.

Chapter 8 – Bump in the Road

It was a short ride to Uncle Bump's apartment and Benny noticed that his neighborhood was dramatically different from Unc's. The rows of apartment buildings down the street each had a few patches of grass in front of them. There were a lot of people congregating on the sidewalks and sitting on the stoops of the apartment buildings and houses on the street.

A group of older men stood outside of the corner store drinking out of brown paper bags, and arguing about which baseball and softball teams were the best in the city. Streams of young children ran up and down the street playing a game of *Tag*.

As Unc pulled up to the red brick apartment building where Uncle Bump had lived for nearly ten years, Unc recalled to Benny the day that he offered to help Uncle Bump move his furniture into his apartment.

"I still remember the pain I had in my back lifting Bump's heavy furniture up those stairs to the top floor," Unc frowned as if feeling the pain again. "The only thing your Uncle Bump could say was I owe you one, brother! I still say he owes me more than *one* for all of that hard labor!" Unc emphasized firmly as his eyes widened.

Benny laughed out loud, enjoying the light moment with Unc.

"Yep, I can hear Uncle Bump now, laughing and telling you to stop being a siss. . ."

Unc abruptly ended the playful exchange by announcing, "Well, let's get you settled in before it gets too late."

Unc quickly took the keys out of the car ignition and reached over to pull up the back door latch.

"Cool!" Benny exclaimed as he pulled his duffle bag from the back seat.

"I'll meet you up there," Unc said.

He looked out of the window and took a deep breath to prepare for the long climb to his brother's apartment. Benny quickly dragged his duffle bag up the stairs toward Uncle Bump's apartment.

"Number 311," Benny whispered as he knocked on Uncle Bump's door. While staring at the closed black metal door, Benny breathed heavily and wiped the sweat from his forehead. He could hear Uncle Bump's heavy footsteps approaching the door.

"Hey, Benny boy," Uncle Bump, greeted Benny, "So, you ready to hang out with me for a little while?"

"Yep, I sure am," Benny responded, grinning hard.

Uncle Bump's tall muscular stature made him look like the ideal paratrooper that he was. Serving in the United States Army, he had no fear when he had to jump out of airplanes and fought in the war in another country. He was Benny's idea of a real life hero. His golden brown skin shimmered against the bright hallway light that peaked through his apartment doorway.

"Come in and put your bag in the back bedroom. That's where you'll be sleeping," Uncle Bump chuckled with his robust laugh and gave Benny a gentle slap on his back.

Unc finally reached the apartment door.

"Hello, brother," Unc called into the apartment in his formal voice as he slowly closed the door behind him.

"Hey," Uncle Bump replied. "Come on in. How ya been big bro'?"

"Pretty good, pretty good," Unc said, finding his way to the sofa where he sat down to catch his breath.

"I see things haven't changed much around here," Unc said. "I guess it would be too much trouble for those young men to stay off of the corner, get a job or do something productive with their time."

"Yeah, everything is peachy around here, man," Uncle Bump replied ignoring Unc's critical observation of the poor condition of the neighborhood. "Everyone knows everybody and you know *everybody* knows me!" Uncle Bump boasted.

He slapped himself on the chest and belted out a loud laugh that caused Benny to snicker quietly in the back bedroom as he eavesdropped on their conversation. He glanced at the shelves against the bedroom wall displaying all Uncle Bump's high school baseball trophies and military medals.

"You know Benny is really excited about coming to live with you, but you have to keep him on schedule with his studies," Unc urged, ignoring his brother's boasting about his popularity.

"Oh, I know you've set some *high* standards for him, man, but I'll try my best to keep him on track. I've even made arrangements to have my lady friend fix him a home-cooked meal every now and then!" Uncle Bump replied giving Unc a playful wink.

Unc rolled his eyes and turned to give his brother one of his familiar smirks.

"By the way, we need to make a decision pretty soon about what we're going to do with the money that we received from the sale of Pop's land. Part of that money should be used for college savings for Benny of course," Unc said. His bass voice engulfed the small space of Uncle Bump's living room.

"Yeah, I agree, but Lena may have another idea about how to spend her share of the money. You know she'll probably want to buy a new wardrobe for herself first. That girl has got to look good," Uncle Bump said with his usual light-hearted laugh.

Unc's look of disgust didn't change as he jumped to his feet.

"I don't think she should get *a dime,* since she didn't lift a finger to help us with Pop, and *she's* the one who lived with him!" Unc stated matter of factly. And she sure hasn't done much to support Benny!"

Unc's face was now beet red.

Uncle Bump turned toward the back bedroom and noticed the door opened slightly. Benny was pretending to unpack his bag. Uncle Bump motioned to Unc to quickly end the conversation.

Benny shrugged his shoulders as the men's voices suddenly went silent. He sat on the edge of the bed to peer out of the bedroom window.

"Man, I sure wish things *were* different for me, he whispered as he slowly shook his head. "Why does everything have to be so complicated?" he mumbled to himself.

"Benny, I'm about to leave now," Unc called back toward the bedroom.

"We'll continue this conversation a little later, Unc said pointing his finger at Uncle Bump.

"Alright, bro', try not to get all worked up about this stuff. I'll make sure Benny is taken care of while you're gone, but we may not do all of that church stuff, though," Uncle Bump said as he chuckled again giving another wink to Unc.

Unc frowned even harder in response. As Benny walked out of the bedroom toward him to extend his hand for a handshake Unc abruptly changed his facial expression.

"Have a safe trip, Unc, Benny said. I'll make sure that I do all of my chores and stay on top of my school work while you're gone."

"I'm trusting that you will, son," Unc replied, "Just remember to mind Uncle Bump. I'll write you as soon as we get settled in our apartment." Unc firmly shook Benny's hand and patted him on the back.

"I know you'll do well," Unc continued in his approving principal's tone.

Benny walked Unc to his car. He stood on the sidewalk as he watched him drive off.

"Yes!" Benny exclaimed as if he had been suddenly released from a head lock.

"Uncle Bump," Benny called up to his open apartment window, "I'm about to take a walk around the block."

"Sure, just make your way back in here before it gets too late," Uncle Bump called back as he chuckled and pointed to his wristwatch. "Don't you go gettin' into no trouble with those rough-neck alley cats either. I ain't got time to kick nobody's butt tonight," he continued as he punched his fist into the palm of his hand.

Benny laughed and inhaled deeply as he began to appreciate the freedom that Uncle Bump was giving him.

"I'm gonna like this – no rules for eight months!" he blurted out as he walked down the sidewalk.

Just then a slim figure was standing right in front of him grinning widely.

"Benjamin Turner? What are you doing in *my* neighborhood?" A familiar female voice asked.

"Hey, Hattie Bea, I didn't know you lived near my Uncle," Benny stammered.

He tried to act as if he hadn't already found out from Teddy where she had moved.

"I've been living around here since last month when they messed up our old neighborhood. You know it was really sad to see so many houses being knocked down. And I cried when they knocked down your grandfather's house," Hattie Bea said rubbing her greasy hands down the front of her blue flowered cotton dress.

"Come on, Hattie Bea!" A chorus of young squeaky voices yelled from behind her.

"I'm comin!" she yelled back. "Got to go finish combing all of them nappy heads over there! So, I guess I'll see you next week at school," Hattie said.

"Yep, I'll be there," Benny smiled, glancing into her dark brown eyes.

"Okay, well I'll see you then," Hattie Bea said, walking backward toward the front stoop of her house.

Her four sisters sat impatiently, waiting their turn to get their hair braided.

Benny's heart pounded as he thought about seeing Hattie Bea everyday walking through the hallways at Cardozo.

"I can't wait to carry Miss Garrison's books to class," Benny whispered aloud. "Man, she sure is looking good!"

He stood like a statue watching her as she walked back to her house. Little kids ran around him as they continued their game of *Tag* on the sidewalk. Hattie resumed her position sitting in a chair as she grabbed sections of thick bushy hair to braid. Her sisters screamed and yelled in pain with each stroke of the hair brush.

Benny recalled that she hardly ever hung out when he was living with Pop-Pop. Since she was the oldest of five girls, she had naturally taken on the role of helping her mom take care of her younger sisters while she worked two cleaning jobs.

His intense concentration on Hattie Bea was interrupted as an annoying voice called out his name.

"Benny Turner. Benny, the fake-me-out peanut-head baseball player from Southwest, Turner," the voice echoed down the long crowded street.

A loud outburst of laughter followed behind the voice to encourage the squeaky voice to continue the verbal assault.

Benny walked slowly toward the figure that was now slinking sideways in a choreographed walk toward him from the middle of the street. He recognized the face as Arthur Kaye, one of his biggest rival pitchers from another boys' club in the Walter Johnson Baseball League.

Arthur was notorious for criticizing Benny's pitching skills. He walked ahead of the group of guys hanging out at the corner store toward Benny.

"Arthur. It's *always* great to see you, even if it is in my uncle's *cool* neighborhood," Benny responded sarcastically.

"It's good to see you, too, *Hinny Penny* Benny. So, you hangin' 'round here these days? I know it's hard to know what team you're playing on 'cause you've lived in just about every part of town at one time or another."

Arthur looked back at the boys standing behind him awaiting a loud roar of laughter in response. He knew how to strike the sensitive nerves of his rivals, but Benny never seemed to react.

"Sounds like you're jealous, man. Maybe you should get out more yourself," Benny sharply responded with a smirk. "In fact, maybe it would do you good to hang with folks who aren't all obnoxious like you," Benny continued.

"Oh, so you've got a little trash talkin'," Arthur responded in a more serious squeaky tone.

Calling back toward the corner, he said, "Fellas, you hear this punk trying to talk like he's something, he ain't . . ."

"Nothin', Benny quickly interrupted, "Man, you say the same ol' tired stuff all the time. You need to get some new material, and get a new pitching game, too."

A chorus of "OOO" ricocheted across the street in response.

Benny breathed deeply as his heart pounded wildly under his cotton t-shirt. His hands were sweating as he prepared for a physical confrontation. He couldn't believe that he had the nerve to respond to Arthur's insults, but it felt good.

"You know what, Turner," Arthur shouted at him as he stood in front of Benny on the sidewalk, "Let's see how much trash you talk when you don't make the Cardozo baseball team this year. You don't have what it takes to make it to the next level," Arthur continued.

Benny expected Arthur to comment about his ability to make the Cardozo baseball team, which would be Dunbar's only serious competition this year among the four Black high schools in the city. Only Cardozo and Dunbar were recognized for having strong athletes.

Benny took another deep breath as he remembered one of the few instructions that Uncle Bump gave him, which was to stay away from the alley cats in the neighborhood. Even though Arthur didn't live in the neighborhood, he would still have to deal with Arthur's cousins for the next eight months.

"I guess we'll just have to wait and see what happens in the spring, won't we?" Benny replied.

He abruptly turned to head back to Uncle Bump's apartment building. This time he walked with sharp and deliberate steps, instead of shuffling his feet knowing he had everyone's attention, *especially* Hattie Bea.

"Yeah, we will, and I'll make sure that I wave to you and the other spectators sitting in the stands," Arthur snickered as he waved his hand high over his head.

Benny didn't respond. He glanced over to Hattie Bea and called out, "See *you* at school."

Benny rolled over toward the bright light shining through the bedroom window. He smiled as he thought about hanging out with Uncle Bump at the baseball field today.

"Benny boy," Uncle Bump called into his room, "You ready to hit the field before the game?"

Uncle Bump was serious about practicing before his games. Today, he would let Benny tag along with him, which meant that Benny didn't have to get dressed up in a suit and tie to go to church.

Benny quickly washed up and got dressed. He hurried to the living room as he watched Uncle Bump gather his equipment. The two prepared for the walk to the ball field four blocks from Uncle Bump's apartment building.

The hustle of families walking in the opposite direction toward the church down the street reminded Benny of his absence from Sunday school.

"Unc wouldn't like this one bit," he smirked.

"Walk lively, now," Uncle Bump called back to Benny.

He carried his long duffle bag in one hand allowing the wooden bats and softballs to rattle inside, while he clutched his large baseball glove under his arm. His black polyester pants with a bright white stripe running down the side of each leg tightly wrapped his long slender legs underneath. Benny had to take long strides to keep up.

"I'm with ya," Benny called back.

Benny tried not to look awkward as he walked in Uncle Bump's shadow.

As they reached the fence of the dirt field, Uncle Bump began rambling instructions to Benny about game day protocol.

"As soon as you walk onto the field, take note of your playing field. Don't waste time trying to look pretty, get yourself mentally in the game, long before the game even starts," Uncle Bump said as he had suddenly transformed into Benny's baseball coach.

"Okay," Benny replied. He walked away from Uncle Bump and placed his baseball glove onto his left hand.

Uncle Bump unzipped his long duffle bag and unpacked his set of light-colored wooden bats. The low hollow sound of the bats slapping against each other as they hit the ground revealed how heavy they were.

Uncle Bump continued with his instructions.

"Now, let me see if you can hit any of *my* pitches," Uncle Bump said, as he motioned to Benny to take his spot at home plate.

"Which bat should I use?" Benny stared at the row of six bats that Uncle Bump had lined neatly on the ground.

"Whatever you think you can handle," Uncle Bump said as he pantomimed a few pitches.

"Okay, I think I'll use the one with the red handle," Benny called out.

"Alright, don't hurt yourself," Uncle Bump warned.

"That's a pretty heavy bat, but it's got a lot of punch!"

Benny took his spot at home plate swinging the heavy bat slowly above his head until he forced it to stop. Uncle Bump held his large leather glove in front of his face before releasing a pitch that Benny barely saw coming.

"Whoa!" Benny shouted. "That was fast!"

"Yeah, that's why it's called fast-pitch softball. This is good practice to get you ready for baseball," Uncle Bump said. "If you can throw this big softball fast, just think what you can do with a little baseball!"

"While you're standing on that pitcher's mound you need to size up the batter." If he's short, your strike zone is low and if he's tall, you know you have to pitch toward the middle."

Benny nodded his head in response while listening intensely to Uncle Bump's instructions.

"Alright, now give me one," Uncle Bump yelled out.

Benny put the leather glove to his face and stared at Uncle Bump's tall body crouched in the batting position. With two quick whirls, the ball whizzed right pass Uncle Bump's bat.

"I think you just threw a strike on your first pitch, my man!" Uncle Bump called to Benny. Chuckling with amazement, he said, "Try that again."

Benny took his stance and pitched the ball again. This time, Uncle Bump took a wild swing at the ball.

"Shucks!" I just knew I had that one," he yelled as he laughed aloud.

"You ready?" Benny asked before he let the third pitch bolt from his hand.

"Got D - - Dang, boy! Who taught you how to pitch like that?" Uncle Bump burst out into one of his robust laughs as he walked toward Benny. If you pitch like that, you shouldn't have *no* problem making the Cardozo team in the spring!" Uncle Bump exploded.

Benny responded with a wide smile as Uncle Bump emphasized his approval by walking over to Benny and tapping him on the butt.

Uncle Bump motioned to Benny to walk toward him on home plate.

"Son, I think you've got natural talent. Pop-Pop really did a good job training you."

"Yeah, he did," Benny said solemnly.

"I know things haven't been the best for you the past few years, but you've got to know that you have family who love you," Uncle Bump continued.

Uncle Bump wiped away a tear before it could reach his cheek. Benny stared at him for a moment before responding.

"Yeah-- I know," Benny sighed.

The two walked over to the bench and talked while Uncle Bump waited for the rest of his teammates to arrive.

"So, what do you think about starting high school this year?" Uncle Bump asked, while untying and tightly retying his cleats.

"I'm kinda excited," Benny replied, kicking dirt speckled with broken pieces of green and clear glass into a small mound. "I know I'll be okay with my classes, but I'm not sure about fitting in with the Cardozo kids."

"Cardozo kids ain't no different from Armstrong kids, Dunbar kids, or Phelps kids. Y'all ain't nothin' but a bunch of youngin's trying to get some smarts so you can make something of yourselves. Don't forget that!" Uncle Bump firmly stated.

Uncle Bump looked Benny right in the eyes as if issuing a command, but quickly lightened the moment by flashing a playful boyish smile.

"Yeah, I guess you're right," Benny replied throwing the softball up and catching it in his glove.

———————————

The excitement and energy around the ball field changed from a quiet laid back lull to loud voices and chatter of the growing crowd as they began arriving for the game. Women and men of all sizes scrambled to squeeze into small spots, as one row after another of the wooden bleachers filled.

The stands of vendors lined the outside of the fence surrounding the ball field with make-shift metal grills. Heated rows of chicken and ribs sizzled and caused thick clouds of smoke to create a mouth-watering aroma across the nostrils of everyone who walked by.

The most popular vendor was the Candy Lady who was known by all of the neighborhood children. She sold all of their favorite penny candies, bubble gum and huge dill pickles floating in the green juice of large glass jars. They all swarmed around her table laughing and making requests for their favorite treats.

Benny looked away from the activity on the field to focus on Uncle Bump as he responded to people constantly whistling and calling out his name.

"Hey, Edgie Bump!" a woman's voice called out from the bleachers.

"See ya, Bump!" a man yelled from behind the fence.

"Edgie!" another woman's voice called out.

Benny grinned as he recalled the story behind why Uncle Bump was given the nickname, Edgie. People called gave him the name to symbolize his daring personality and cutting *edge* performance on the field.

Soon the two teams assembled on each side of home plate. The field that was dominated by pockets of black and white colored uniforms bearing the word *Stonewalls* stitched in bold lettering across the back of each player. A solid white stripe ran down the outside of each pant leg. Each wearing a black baseball cap with the letter *S* stitched in the center. The crunch of their black cleats digging into the dirt left behind a trail of small dots in the ground.

The black and white colors were now balanced out by a steady stream of navy blue and golden yellow uniforms with the team name *Twangers* stitched on the back of their shirts and bright yellow stripes down their pants. The player's navy blue baseball caps were highlighted with a golden yellow letter *T* in the middle.

As both teams arrived, the players smugly threw their duffle bags underneath their wooden benches. The impact caused a loud clanging of the bats that echoed across the field. In precision, they trotted onto the field as another round of cheers erupted from their fans.

"Get 'em, Boogie!" one of the vendors screamed across the field.

"I see you, George!" an older man shouted.

"Let's go Twangers!" a chorus of kids' voices cried out.

One call after another intensified as the volume of cheers from the crowd for their favorite players got louder. Bets were being taken in another corner from the men determined to make money from their predictions of who would win today's game.

Uncle Bump stuck out his chest like a rooster approaching a hen house as he prepared for the start of the game. He pulled each arm up over his head and back across his chest; and glanced at Benny to give him a quick wink.

Benny cheered him on, "Alright, Uncle Bump!" This stirred up another wave of chants from the crowd.

"Come on, Twangers!"

"Go get 'em, Stonewalls!"

The teammates paired up to throw the softball back and forth, swing their bats and sit on the ground to stretch their legs. Benny recognized all of the pre-game rituals that would signal the beginning of an exciting rivalry between two softball teams in the city.

"Let's go, Stonewalls!" Benny yelled in his loudest voice.

The team huddled to say a prayer, while the umpire took his place behind home plate.

"Yeah, go, Stonewalls!" a familiar voice echoed from the crowd behind Benny. It was Hattie Bea clapping her hands with excitement as her eyes connected with Benny's. They both exchanged a vibrant smile.

Excitement reached its peak as the umpire commanded the crowd's attention, and yelled, "Play ball!"

Chapter 9 - A Sense of Purpose

Benny walked across the baseball field shooing swarms of nets that formed suspended wavy screens along his path. A tall stalky man with thick black square glasses stood in the distance holding a clipboard in his hand, barking out instructions to the boys that had already begun warming up for the tryout process.

One boy that Benny recognized was an eleventh-grader named Butch who looked like a tree stump barely able to run the bases.

"That Butch ain't gonna make it home before his time is up," Benny chuckled to himself.

Benny knew how the speed drill went. If you couldn't run the bases in under 60 seconds, you were considered too slow.

"Come on, son," Coach Porter barked, "you can't go no faster than that?"

Butch stopped mid-way to home plate, looked in the direction of Coach Porter and blurted out, "Forgot this mess man, I'm tired!"

Coach Porter took slow steps toward Butch's position on the field and placed his hands on his hips.

"Tired? Hey, Coach Lewis, Did you hear what his boy said?" Coach Porter stared at Butch.

"Boy, you just got out here, how in the world are you *tired*?" Coach Porter continued.

His stern bass voice bounced from one end of the field to the other smacking Benny's eardrum.

Butch hung his head and plopped his body onto the grass.

"What am I doing?" Benny whispered to himself as he looked at Butch's defeated face, "Coach Porter sounds like a bulldog. He ain't trying to pick new guys for his team. I bet his team is already set."

Just then Pop-Pop's voice rang in his head as if he were standing right beside him. "Don't you ever forget that you've got everything you need inside of ya to *make* life fair."

Benny took a deep breath as he walked toward the bench where Coach Porter was standing. Trying out for the *Cardozo Clerks* baseball team was a major step for Benny. He would have rather tried out for Armstrong or Phelps, where he would have less competition, but those schools were on the other side of town.

By attending Cardozo, he would prepare to become an office worker in the Federal government - one of the largest employers in the city. Every Black student living in Washington, DC was strongly encouraged to graduate from high school and get a *good* government job if they weren't able to go to into the military or attend college.

College had not been on Benny's mind, but Unc made college a part of just about every conversation he had with Benny as the best way to avoid being poor.

Benny never had to try out for any of the neighborhood teams, because most of the baseball coaches knew that he came from a family of great ball players. However, now his baseball skills would be put to the test.

Coach Porter was a dark-skinned stocky man wearing a white cotton t-shirt that seemed to be painted onto his body. Those who knew him said he wore his baseball cap low over his forehead to either shield his eyes from the sun or hide his bloodshot eyes from his players.

Coach Porter called for Benny to step forward from the line of 20 boys who signed up and were eager for a chance to demonstrate their skills. Benny's heart pounded hard underneath his navy blue t-shirt.

"What's your name, son?" Coach Porter asked as if questioning a suspect.

"Ben--Benny Turner, sir," Benny stuttered.

"Well, you're next. What position do you think you can play?" Coach Porter continued in his questioning tone.

"I'm a good pitcher, but I've also played short stop for the Walter Johnson League . . ."

"Pitcher?" Coach Porter interrupted. "I definitely want to see what you've got. But let me see if you've got any speed first. Run the bases for me when I give you the signal," Coach Porter motioned to Benny to take his place at home plate.

Coach Porter raised his left hand and reset his stopwatch with the right. As his left hand lowered, he yelled, "Go!"

Benny briefly hesitated as he waited for him to say the usual 'Ready- Set'. But this was high school, so he figured that was for little kids. He pushed his legs to move faster and faster as his heart pounded and his eyes focused reaching first base. He propelled himself toward second, and with greater momentum pushed his body toward third. He leaped across home plate with Coach Porter snapping the stopwatch behind him.

"52 seconds! Boy! You've got a little speed. Shortstop just might work for you," said Coach Porter.

As the next boy lined up to get his turn, Benny thought back to 1947 when he was just 10 years old. He and Pop-Pop sat at the kitchen table eating fried chicken and listening to the Dodger's game on Pop-Pop's radio. The voice of the announcer was yelling "*Jackie Robinson has just made Major League Baseball history*!"

Pop-Pop was yelling even louder, "that Black man done hit a home run in the Majors! Shoot, we can do anything now, boy!"

At that moment, Benny remembered thinking that there was hope for Black boys in DC; and everywhere in America, because Jackie Robinson had surpassed the wealth of talent that the Negro League teams promoted. He made it in the big leagues playing on a White baseball team.

Benny looked across the baseball field and said to himself, "I can do it, too. I'm gonna make this team!"

"Alright, son, let's see what kind of pitching game you've got," Coach Porter called out to Benny.

"Okay, Coach, I'm ready," Benny replied.

Benny took one long swallow of the little spit that remained in his mouth. He wound up his arm to throw a few practice pitches to the catcher, a tenth-grader named Wookie.

Moe Bolden, the team's star hitter, grabbed one of the dark-colored wooden bats and began swinging it back and forth in front of him. As he held the bat above his head, he anxiously waited for the chance to smack the ball into the outfield.

Benny focused on Moe's strike zone and suddenly released his first pitch with a burst of power.

"Strike!" Coach Lewis yelled out with a grin on his face.

"Better keep your eye on the ball, Moe."

"Looks like we may have ourselves a real pitcher," Coach Porter joked.

"That boy ain't got nothin' on me, Coach," Moe replied with a furious frown on his face.

He shuffled the dirt from side to side with his cleats and he got back into his stance determined to hit the next ball.

"Oh, this is gonna be sweet, Benny whispered into his glove, as he prepared to deliver the next lightning fast pitch across the diamond.

"Strike two!" Coach Lewis yelled again.
This time he put both hands on his hips and he stared at Benny for a moment.

"Hey, Benny, you wouldn't happen to be related to Fred and Edgie Bump Turner?" Coach Lewis asked.

"Yes, sir," Benny replied with a slight grin on his face. "That's my grandpa *and* my uncle."

"Moe, you might as well go sit down, son 'cause that boy is about to strike you out!" Coach Lewis whispered to Moe.

He motioned wildly to Coach Porter to come over to the batting cage.

"Porter, this boy may be just what we need. Anybody who can strike Moe out is *good,*" Coach Lewis exclaimed trying to control his excitement.

"Coach, give me another chance," Moe replied sharply, "I'm gonna smack this next one so hard that little Benny won't know what happened to it!"

Moe's practice swings had greater force, as he swung wildly into the mild breeze that lingered over the field.

Without any further warm-up, Benny delivered another pitch, which seemed to whiz in a straight line across the diamond and just under Moe's violent swing.

"Strike three!" Coach Lewis yelled. "Son, you've got a mean pitch," he screamed out to Benny.

Moe slammed his bat to the ground in disgust.

Coach Lewis turned toward Coach Porter and said with excitement, "You know that's Fred Turner's grandson and Edgie Bump's nephew out there. That boy has got the Turner gift and we're gonna open that gift *up* to put a hurtin' on Dunbar this year!"

Coach Porter chuckled, "Okay, now hold tight, Lew. He still has to prove himself under pressure in a real game against some fierce opponents, including Arthur Kaye. That boy's pitching game ain't nothing to sneeze at either. The two of them pitching against each other would make for an interesting season, no doubt," Coach Porter continued.

"Arthur Kaye?" Benny whispered to himself.

He overheard Coach Porter mention the name of the one person he despised.

"I have to prove myself against that puffed up trash talker once and for all," Benny stated as he recalled the insults Arthur loved to hurl at him.

Coach Porter motioned for the group of boys to gather around the bench.

"Alright, boys, that's it for the tryouts. We'll post the names for this year's roster in the main hall tomorrow. We'll see who's gonna be playing for the Clerks this year," he continued.

———————————

Benny could hardly wait for Uncle Bump to get home. He could hear his bass voice exchanging stats of his favorite team with the men on the corner. Soon, he could hear his boots stomping up the stairs toward the apartment. As he turned the knob to enter the apartment Benny could barely control his excitement.

"Guess what happened at tryouts today, Uncle Bump!" Benny's grin overpowered his face.

"Well, good evening to you, too!" Uncle Bump interrupted. "Now, tell me, what happened that's got you so riled up!" Uncle Bump smiled with his normal cool tone.

"Coach Porter was barking at all of us, trying to make us feel like we didn't have a chance to make the team. But when he put *me* on the mound, I struck out Moe Bolden. *The* Moe Bolden who hardly ever misses a hit!" Benny was spitting and barely able to catch his breath as he described the ease of striking Moe out.

"Wow, that's pretty good," Uncle Bump replied, as he rubbed his hand over his head.

He watched as Benny's smile grew wider and wider across his face. He couldn't help thinking about how much sadness he had observed Benny overcome past few months. The sight of him being happy caused Uncle Bump's eyes to water.

"Yep, I threw that ball right down the middle of the strike zone. Just like you and Pop-Pop showed me. Those three strikes were easy!" Benny shouted.

He was now pacing wildly back and forth across the living room floor as if he were a dog begging to go outside.

"Coach Porter said that he's gonna put up the names of everybody who made the team in the main hall tomorrow. Man, I just know I made it! I'm gonna be a Cardozo Clerk!" Benny jumped up pounding his fist into his hand.

"Be careful now," Uncle Bump, chuckled, "You don't want to injure that pitching hand before the first game."

Benny let out a hearty laugh as he ran into his bedroom to relish in the moment.

"Maybe we can celebrate tomorrow with some ribs from Johnnie Boy's for dinner," Uncle Bump suggested still grinning about Benny's new sense of joy.

"Sounds *goooood* to me," Benny called back enthusiastically.

Chapter 10 - Making A Mark

The school year was almost over before Unc returned from Europe to reunite with a more mature Benny. Benny had challenged himself to do well academically and athletically. He considered school a place of acceptance and recognition, and a place to escape the prejudice and discrimination that had become an acceptable way of life for many Blacks in D.C. and across the country.

A local news article described the skills of a little known Black high school baseball pitcher from Southwest who managed to put Cardozo in the spotlight by striking out multiple batters in every game he played.

Unc had bought all of the papers from the corner store to share with Benny and his friends. As he walked toward the group of boys goofing off on the playground, the horseplay quickly ceased as Unc approached.

"Greetings young men," Unc said, in his formal tone.

"Hello, Mr. Turner," they each replied respectfully.

"Hey Unc," Benny responded after giving Pudge another playful punch on his shoulder.

"Well, I thought you all would like to read something I found in today's paper about someone that you *all* know," Unc announced.

He handed a copy of the newspaper folded back to the Sports section to each of the boys smirking at Benny as he handed the last paper to him.

"Man, that's me—that's my name!" Benny exclaimed as he read aloud the news article featuring his name in black and white.

"Yes, you've made the paper, son," Unc grinned as he read along in his own copy of the paper. "You sound like one of the players in the Majors. One day, we'll be reading about Ben 'Cap' Turner in the White papers, too!" he continued.

Unc's bass voice boomed from the playground and down the street as he encouraged Benny and his friends to take turns reading the article aloud imitating the voice of a sports announcer:

June 3, 1952 -- The Cardozo Clerks capitalized on a pair of errors by the Dunbar Tide in the fourth inning and settled a hurling duel between Benny (Cap) Turner and Arthur (Tree) Kaye with a

1-0 triumph over the Tide, Thursday in the Clerks'

Stadium.

"Benny I think the first thing you should do when you make it big is change the name of our sports teams. *Clerks just* sound so weak!" Shoo-Shoo exclaimed.

"Yeah, I'll make a note of that," Benny chuckled.

"Check this out, Kirby continued:

Kaye, a gangling 6-foot, 3-inch right-hander, hurled a one-hit performance, but saw his best pitching effort go to waste in the fourth inning on consecutive miscues by Hadley Latimer and Joseph Jones.

"Man, that dude couldn't hang with you Benny, he ain't have nothin' on you!" Shoo-Shoo shouted.

Pudge continued reading the article in his high-pitched voice:

Catcher Wayne Miller was safe when third baseman Latimer threw wide to first base. Miller advanced to second on the throw promptly stole third base, and romped home with what proved the winning run when second baseman Jones fumbled a hot liner by Cook.

Therein lies the story of the scoring. The real story is one of the strong determination of two former junior high school rivals now, trying to out pitch each other again.

Kaye, mixing side-arm and overhand deliveries effectively limited Cardozo to a single hit that being a double by Kyle May in the second inning. Showing brilliant control, Kaye fanned eight batters, walked one and hit one opposing hitter in losing a heart-breaking tilt, his third

setback in four games.

Benny chimed in to read the next section.

Turner, who attended Banneker Junior High

School last year, whiffed 12 batters over the seven-

inning stint, but was tagged for four scattered

bingles.

Kirby chimed in, "Dang, Benny, you took

down 12 batters, you are the baddest pitcher

Cardozo has ever seen!"

Benny shrugged his shoulders as if it weren't

a big deal, as Unc insisted on continuing to get to

the end of the article.

The tiny right-hander whose sinker gave

Dunbar considerable trouble throughout the contest,

walked two Tide batters, and was in the hottest

water in the final inning.

Jones, seeking to redeem himself for the costly error in the fourth inning, doubled down the left field foul line to open the inning.

Turner, posting his fourth victory in five games fanned Yelder, and then forced Crockett to pop up. Reggie Taylor lined out to Henry Burrell in centerfield to end the game.

The contest played amidst threatening showers before some 300 fans, was the sixth triumph in seven games for the Clerks, and the seventh setback in 12 turns at bat for Dunbar.

"You've had quite an impressive start playing for Cardozo. Just make sure you keep your grades up as well," Unc admonished as he gave Benny a quick wink of encouragement and pat on the back.

"Yep, that's my plan," Benny beamed with pride.

Chapter 11 Junior Love

Benny successfully completed his first two years at Cardozo. Now, he was beginning his eleventh grade year and officially an upper classman.

The first period bell was about to ring, as he took his books out of his locker. Benny noticed a subtle fragrance of roses flow past his face. He knew that his locker was nowhere near the school's rose garden, but the overpowering floral scent only got stronger.

As he shut his locker, he glanced to his right to see the key to the mystery standing three lockers away--Hattie Bea. Her jet black hair that shined like a brand new record album as the ceiling lights reflected off of her bangs. Her eyes were perfectly almond-shaped and magnetic.

"Hattie Bea?" Benny called out to the young girl as she struggled to open her locker.

"Hey, Benny. I'm gonna be tardy in a minute, unless I can get this stupid locker open!" Hattie responded abruptly, barely glancing at Benny

"Here, let me help you," Benny replied as he rammed his shoulder against the metal locker to release the latch.

"Thanks, I sure appreciate that," Hattie replied as she grabbed her books, slammed her locker shut.

She whisked down the hallway as her blue dress swayed behind her leaving a trail of her floral fragrance. Benny watched her image shrink smaller and smaller into the distance as he inhaled deeply to savor the refreshing scent she left behind.

As Benny approached Mr. Duval's class, a whiff of the familiar rose scent drew his attention to the second row of typewriters.

"Hattie is in my typing class!" Benny said under her breath.

"Hey, Hattie, I see you again," Benny stuttered as he took his seat on the fourth row directly behind Hattie's seat.

"Oh, hey, again," Hattie replied.

She was pre-occupied with stacking her books under her chair.

"I see we have the *same* class at the *same* time," Benny replied, displaying one of his widest smiles.

"Yep, looks that way." Hattie replied cutting her eyes away as Mr. Duval brought the class to order.

Benny could barely focus on the typing lesson as he stared at the back of Hattie's glistening black hair with the strands of her hair smoothly wrapped into a pony tail touching the base of her milk chocolate neck. Her cotton dress had crisply pressed pleats that draped across the top of her back. The tiny floral pattern rose up and down with each breath.

"This is gonna be a good year," Benny whispered as he cracked his knuckles straight out in front of him to prepare for a typing drill on his typewriter.

Months passed as Benny's focus on his new love continued to grow. His desire to spend time with Hattie began to affect his ability to prepare for his third baseball season.

Coach Porter had noticed Benny's lack of effort during practice. During the last practice before the game against Dunbar, his pitches were off the mark.

Even though Benny knew that the team had to prepare for the biggest game of the season, he couldn't get Hattie off of his mind.

"Hey, Turner," Coach Porter called out.

Benny held his glove toward his chest and ran toward home plate.

"Yeah, Coach?" he answered with his eyes stretched open.

"What's going on, son?" Coach Porter asked putting his hand on his hip and staring right into Benny's eyes as he began questioning him.

"The last few practices, you haven't had any strike outs. Is everything alright at home?" Coach Porter asked as he looked over the top of his glasses.

"Yeah, everything is fine, Coach," Benny replied hesitantly, looking down at his cleats.

"Now, you know you can talk to me about anything, right? Coach Porter reassured Benny, as he pressed his heavy hand on Benny's shoulder.

Just then, a voice yelled from the outfield.

"Benny's got a girlfriend, Coach! That's why he ain't got no pitching game!"

Benny's eyes sharply looked into Coach Porter's face as if in terror that his secret was now exposed.

"Girlfriend, huh?" Coach Porter blurted out.

"You know girls can be a world of trouble to an athlete, son. You may need to put your love on hold until we make it to the championship game-- for the good of your team. But I'll leave that decision up to you, son," Coach Porter said.

Benny glanced at Coach Porter's face, but already knew what he planned to do. He folded his glove under one arm and pulled his cap down on his forehead.

"Oh I'll be ready," Benny murmured under his breath.

He grabbed his duffle bag tightly in his hand, and jogged off the field.

Chapter 12 - The Championship Game (June 6, 1954)

Cardozo and Dunbar managed to eliminate Phelps and Armstrong in the playoff games. Now, both teams were heading to the Championship game.

The Clerks' stadium steadily filled with fans from Cardozo and Dunbar vivaciously chanting their schools' fight songs. Calling out the names of their school mascots was like a verbal duel—

"Clerks!"

"Tide!"

"Clerks Go to Work!"

"Tide Got Pride!"

Vendors were set up on both sides of the outside fence drawing crowds to their tables with the smoky aroma of grilled chicken and barbequed ribs stacked up on the grill. A handwritten sign read hung on the fence:

Chicken	*$1.50*
Ribs	*$2.00*
Hot Dogs	*.50*
Soda	*.25*
Chips	*.20*

The rainbow of flavored syrup lined the table where cups of shaved ice were being sold for a nickel. As the purple and white stream of uniforms arrived on the field, the crowd of Clerks fans screamed and yelled out the names of the players.

A deep male voice yelled, "Benny!"

Another high-pitched shriek yelled toward the field, "Petey!"

A chorus of female voices yelled in unison, "Let's

go, Clerks!"

Minutes later, black and red uniforms began to intersperse throughout the field as cheers erupted from the other side of the stands.

"It's time for the Dunbar Tide to shine," a woman called out from the first row.

"Come on, fellas, let's get a win," another voice cried a few rows behind her.

The robust tone of the game announcer's voice welcomed the crowd with an animated introduction:

"Welcome baseball fans to the 5th Annual D.C. Public Schools Baseball Championship game between the Cardozo Clerks and the Dunbar Tide! This intense high school rivalry is being played on one of the hottest days of the year in front of over a thousand fans from around the city."

"We are about to witness the best group of players

taking the field today to battle to the last inning and claim

the rights of being named the 1954 high school all-stars!"

the announcer continued as he yelled into this microphone.

The opportunity to play in the championship

game with scouts from colleges and Minor League

Baseball teams watching only increased the pressure

that Benny felt. Beads of sweat began to rise on his

forehead and slowly dampen the inside brim of his

cap.

Benny glanced around the stadium taking in

the excitement that was building as the fans for both

teams took their places on the wooden bleachers.

Just then he spotted Unc, Uncle Bump and

Mama sitting on the front row. Seated a few rows

behind was Hattie Bea grinning from ear to ear.

Benny shook his head as he noticed Kirby, Shoo-

Shoo, Patch, and Pudge standing near a crowd of boys hovered in a corner of the stadium exchanging money to bet on which team would win the game.

"Hey, Wookie, Benny called to his catcher, "Let's get in a few practice pitches before we knock this game out."

"Ready when you are, Cap," Wookie called back.

Benny pulled each arm across his body and up over his head to prepare to warm up.

"Give me one of those, curve balls," Wookie shouted.

"Check this one out," Benny shouted back.

Turning to his left, Benny placed the glove close to his face as he gripped the ball tight in his right hand. With a single motion, he swung his arm around full circle and released the ball.

"Let's play ball," Umpire Goode yelled.

"Looks like this championship game is about to begin," the announcer proclaimed as his voice echoed across the stadium.

We have Arthur Kaye pitching today for the Tide. He'll be pitching against his rival; Benny 'Cap' Turner for the Clerks," the announcer continued, "The Clerks will begin the game at bat."

As Benny sat on the bench he carefully took notes as he watched Arthur strut out to the mound.

Groups of Dunbar fans responded in unison --

"Go, Tide!'

"Tide Pride!"

An old man bellowed, "Let's get some runs, boys!"

"Watch Moe hit one to the White House!" Pudge called from a spot near the fence.

Arthur tipped his hat as if he were about to put on a one-man show for the crowd.

The announcer described every movement that Arthur made.

"Arthur begins the first inning with a mixed side-arm delivering a powerful over-hand pitch as he establishes his domination of the mound," the announcer said.

Each pitch that Arthur executed seemed to fly away from the Clerks' bats as each batter's attempts to swing or bunt the ball failed.

Arthur drew more confident as the Dunbar fans continued to yell out to encourage him to strike out each batter.

"Kaye has effectively limited the Clerks' ability to get a single hit!" the announcer informed the crowd.

Benny continued to study every twist and turn of Arthur's body until he heard a solid crack of the bat.

"Well, well, well! The Clerks finally have a runner on base! Jerome Wooten hits a sweet one out to left field!" the announcer yelled sarcastically.

The crescendo of his voice into the microphone caused the Clerks' fans to suddenly erupt into screams and yells.

"Keep running, Jerome!" one woman yelled.

"Woo-woo- Wooten!" a chorus of girls called toward the field.

Jerome was encouraged to keep running around the bases.

"A solid throw by left-fielder Mookie Smith, holds Wooten at second," the announcer informed the crowd.

"Moe Bolden is up next. This could be a big break for the Clerks as one of their powerhouse batters takes his place in the batter box! The announcer slowly spoke into the microphone creating anticipation as the crowd waited to see what would happen next.

"Kaye is keeping his eye on Wooten as he prepares to deliver his first pitch to Bolden," the announcer continued.

Arthur rubbed the rim of his cap as he placed his glove behind his back, clasping the ball tightly inside. One step forward, he allowed his right arm to extend forward as the ball released from his hand.

"S-T-R-I-K-E!" the umpire called out as he extended his arm out to the right.

Moe readjusted his stance as he responded to calls from the stands and hand signals from Coach Lewis.

"Come on, Moe hit the ball!" Kirby yelled.

"Do what you do, Moe!" a bass voice called out.

"We need Moe to get a run before Butch gets up to bat," Benny whispered to himself.

Arthur lifted his left leg as he forcefully wound his arm forward to release another fast pitch, but this time Moe's bat connected with a loud hollow crack.

"Go Moe!" Coach Lewis was screaming as he wildly waved for Wooten to run to home plate.

"Alright, Moe, go all the way!" Benny shouted as he leaped up from the bench.

"Wooten taps home and right behind him coming full speed is Moe Bolden! What a wake-up call for the Tide! The Clerks have just scored two runs!" the announcer yelled.

The Clerks fans jumped to their feet and cheered as the two stamped their cleats onto the home plate.

"Next at bat for the Clerks is Butch Fuller. Kaye looks a little disappointed in his performance. I don't think he's gonna allow another hit from the Clerks, folks." the announcer warned.

Butch watched the wrinkles on Kaye's forehead deepen as Arthur stared intently at the catcher's mitt.

As Arthur aimed his throw, the breeze of the ball whizzed by Butch's head and he heard the umpire yell --

"S-T-R-I-K-E!"

Butch kicked dirt on the side of the plate and steadied his bat to prepare for the next pitch.

Arthur peered over his glove and released the ball to cause Butch to swing wildly.

"Strike two!" the umpire motioned with his arm.

"Son, wait for the ball," Coach Porter yelled to Butch.

"Take your time, Butch," Benny yelled.

Arthur wound up a quick pitch before Butch could get back into his batting stance.

"Strike three! You're out!" the umpire dragged out the words.

"Did y'all see that?" the announcer asked the crowd, "Kaye struck like lightning on Fuller and that's the third out for the Clerks. It's the Tide's turn at bat."

"Looks like Turner's coming out to the mound with his game face on. What a game this has turned out to be!"

he shouted into the microphone.

Benny removed his cap as he wiped the sweat from his forehead with the back of his hand.

"Okay, this is it," he called to Wookie.

Wookie nodded his head as he squatted behind home plate and hit his hand into the center of his catcher's mitt to await a couple of practice pitches.

Benny rehearsed Uncle Bump's instructions — 'Focus on throwing the ball right into the middle of the batter's strike zone so it lands right in the middle of the catcher's mitt.'

Spitting into his glove, Benny gripped the ball and threw two fast pitches into Wookie's glove before the first Tide batter took his place in the batter's box.

Benny bowed his head toward his chest; hit the ball into the palm of his glove as he whispered, "This game's for you, Teddy and Pop-Pop."

Stepping up on the mound, Benny stared right past the tall batter and aimed toward the middle of Wookie's glove. He placed his glove in front of his face and he released a powerful fast ball.

"S-T-R-I-K-E!" the umpire yelled.

"Turner's returning the favor on the Tide as his first pitch leaves Bullock stunned at bat!" the announcer joked.

Uncle Bump yelled out, "Come on, Benny, stick it right in the zone! Focus on the zone!"

Unc resisted the urge to yell out to Benny, but clapped his hands as a sign of support. Mama fanned herself with one of the game programs.

"They really need to build some shade over these bleachers for these games," she complained aloud as she patted her nose and forehead with a cotton handkerchief.

No one responded to her complaint as all eyes were focused on the thin image standing on the pitcher's mound. Benny rotated his arm forward until the ball released from his hand like a cannon ball right into the center of Wookie's mitt.

"S-T-R-I-K-E!" the umpire yelled as he motioned with his right arm.

"Whoa! I believe Turner just threw a sinker right past Bullock!" the announcer said in amazement.

"There you go, Benny, that's how we do it, Uncle Bump yelled, "Let's keep it going," as he rapidly clapped his hands.

Benny took a deep breath as he prepared to repeat the same pattern to strike out the Tide batter.

His face grew more intense as his confidence increased with each pitch.

"STRIKE!"

"STRIKE!"

"STRIKE!"

The umpire's voice echoed across the stadium like a parrot. As one batter after another was forced to relinquish their bat and take a seat back on the Tide's bench.

"What are y'all doin' out there?" Arthur screamed at his teammates stomping the ground until a cloud of dirt swirled in front of him.

"Turner is demonstrating his normal control of the ball, striking out three batters in a row. I hope the Tide has an answer to that stellar performance," the announcer yelled into the microphone.

Arthur Kaye jeered at Benny as he jogged past him toward the Clerk bench.

"Your luck's about to run out, Hinny Penny," he called behind Benny.

While still jogging ahead, Benny turned his head slightly to the side to respond to Arthur. "I'm not a *lucky* person, so I guess I'll have to depend on *raw* talent!"

Arthur rolled his eyes and pounded his hand hard into his glove and he barked at his teammates to hold Cardozo to only two runs.

"We didn't come to the Championship to lose, so look alive and get these suckers out," Arthur commanded.

Dunbar's coach, yelled out toward the players as they took the field, "That's right! Arthur can't win the game by himself, fellas. Every man's gotta play his position! We came to win!"

Coach Porter called all of the players into a huddle.

"Now, boys, you've already seen that they've got a pretty weak outfield, so let's connect with the ball and get some more runs! We're gonna win this game, because we have the better team! Do you believe that?" Coach Porter asked with excitement in his voice.

"Yeah!" the players shouted back in unison.

Benny grinned widely as he yelled the loudest.

"Then put your hands in and let's get some more runs!" Coach Porter demanded as he sprayed spit into Wookie's face.

"We've had quite a show from the Clerks in the last inning. Let's see if the Tide can hold the Clerks to two runs," said the announcer.

"Come on little Clerk, let me strike you out right quick," Kaye taunted Tony Davis.

As Arthur stepped forward he pretended to throw the ball high into the air causing Tony to swing at the air.

"Strike one!" the umpire called.

"Kaye just threw a curve ball on Davis," the announcer informed the crowd.

"Ha!" Arthur laughed as he enjoyed humiliating batters.

Benny yelled out to encourage Tony, "Keep your head in the game, Tony, and keep your eye on the ball."

Tony shook his head in response to Benny and looked over toward Coach Lewis who was giving him a hand signal.

Arthur leaned back to give his right arm momentum as he threw the next pitch. Tony turned the bat sideways and tapped the ball so it fell right in front of the pitching mound. Arthur looked stunned as he stumbled to scoop the ball with his glove causing it to flip behind him.

"Davis just bunted the ball!" the announcer belted out.

"Run, Tony!" Coach Porter yelled waving his arms backward and forward.

"You've got it, Tony" Benny called out.

The second baseman called for the ball, but Arthur pushed him out of the way. They both fell to the ground scrambling for ownership of the ball as the coach yelled out to them.

"Get the dang ball and get him out!" the coach screamed.

The intense screams of the Cardozo players propelled Tony to reach the first base bag before Arthur was able to throw the ball.

"Oh my goodness! I don't believe what I just saw. Kaye seems a little frustrated with his team right now, but he can't fight them!" the announcer said in bewilderment.

Benny snickered as he whispered to himself,

"Arthur, it looks like *you* aren't having much luck today."

"Kaye is going to have to pull out all of the stops in this inning if the Tide is going to stop the Clerks!" the announcer emphasized.

Arthur readjusted his cap as he wiped the dirt from his pants.

"That was a lucky hit, but that's the last one," he warned as he stared at the face of the next Clerks' batter, Charlie Garrett.

Charlie swung his hips from side to side as he steadied the bat tightly above his head. Arthur held his glove in front of his face as his eyes connected with his catcher to give him a signal.

"Come on, Charlie," Benny called from the bench.

Arthur stepped up and released a high curved pitch past Charlie.

"BALL!" the umpire shouted.

"Good eye, Charlie!" Benny called again.

"Ball? Arthur questioned. "That was a strike!"

"In all my years, I have never seen a pitcher question the call," the announcer stated, "Kaye may be pitching from the bench if he keeps this up."

"Son, that's the call. It's a ball, now let me do my job," the umpire responded lifting his mask away from his face.

"Okay, Arthur, we don't need to get the umpire riled up," the coach yelled as he walked toward the mound.

"I know what I threw, Coach, and that ball was clearly a strike," Arthur insisted.

Before Arthur could continue his protest, the umpire walked out to the mound motioning for the Dunbar Coach to meet him there.

"Son, you are not demonstrating good sportsmanlike conduct, and your actions are grounds to remove you from the game. Now either you let me call the game as I see it or you sit on the bench and *watch* the remainder of this game," the umpire's muffled bass voice boomed across the stadium.

"Let the kids, play ball!" a voice from the Tide bleachers yelled out.

"Bunch of cheatin' Clerks!" another voice responded to an eruption of applause from the Tide fans.

"The umpire is setting Kaye straight on who's in charge of calling the game," the announcer spoke deeply into the microphone.

"That Arthur thinks he can control everything," Benny said to Wookie.

"Yeah, but I think Ump Goode is about to show him differently," Wookie responded.

"Arthur, you have to control your temper, son," his coach said in response to Umpire Goode's warning.

"Let's see if y'all can win this game without me!" Arthur shouted as he abruptly walked off of the field headed toward the outside of the fence.

"Arthur, don't let them kick you out of the game!" a voice cried out from the Tide bleachers.

"Yeah, they need you, son, hang in there," another voice followed.

Calls and chants from the Tide fans grew louder and louder—

"We want Arthur!"

"We want Arthur!"

Just then, Arthur took his glove off, ripped his shirt open and threw the ball onto the ground.

"Ladies and gentleman, the pitcher for the Tide, Arthur Kaye, has just walked off of the field leaving his team in a lurch! Unbelievable! Simply unbelievable!" the announcer said in amazement. "Back-up pitcher, Al Chapman is going to have to take over for Kaye."

Al nervously warmed up with a couple of practice pitches before Garrett returned to bat. He never imagined that he would ever replace Arthur, especially not in the Championship game.

He tried to mimic Arthur's pitching ritual, but soon learned that he was not ready for what was about to happen.

He took one step to release a slow ball that ended in a loud crack of the bat as the ball sailed over the head of the Tide's center-fielder.

The announcer screamed, "Garrett has just hit a home run for the Clerks! That brings Davis home with Garrett running right behind as the score now sits at 4-0 in favor of the Clerks!

Looks like the Clerks did come to *work*. We may have just witnessed what may be the beginning of the end for the Tide." he continued.

"Yes, we did!" Benny responded looking at the announcer as he clapped his hands together.

"Go, Clerks!" Mama's high-pitched voice screamed out.

"The Clerks *are* number one," Uncle Bump proclaimed.

———————————

As each inning came and went, the momentum of Dunbar's players dwindled as confidence of the Cardozo players got stronger.

They scored one homerun after another. Benny pitched with precision and Al continued to allow Clerks batters on base.

"Folks we are at the bottom of the ninth and the score is a whopping 10-0," the announcer said in disbelief.

The Tide fans steadily began leaving the stadium as defeat became certain.

"Benny 'Cap' Turner has dominated the pitching game," the announcer joked, "And as we near the end of this game, the Tide has yet to get a base hit. Their last hope is Edwards who's at bat, but with two outs. I do believe we are about to wrap this game up," the announcer continued.

Benny raised his glove as he rubbed the ball into the palm. Giving Wookie a nod, he threw his arm forward.

"STRIKE THREE!" the umpire belted out as the last call of the game.

"Benny Turner has just ended this game with one of the fastest fast balls I've *ever* seen! The announcer said as he chuckled, "What an ending to the most unusual Championship game ever!

The Cardozo Clerks are the City Champions for 1954 earning the title as the number one Negro high school team in the Washington, DC–Baltimore area! Thanks to the stellar pitching performance of the Clerks' all-star pitcher Benny 'Cap' Turner, and batting quartet of Wooten, Bolden, Garrett and Davis, the Clerks shut out the Tide with a final score of 10-0!"

Benny leaned his head back to allow the strong rays of the sun rest on his face as the excitement of their victory sunk in. He smiled as he heard Pop-Pop's voice whispering to him, "I'm proud of you, son."

The Clerks team emptied the bench like a herd of wild horses trotting full force toward the pitcher's mound.

"We won!" a female voice cried out.

"We did it!" Coach Porter screamed as he leaped into the air.

"Benny whipped their butts!" yet another male voice screamed from across the field.

Unc, Uncle Bump, Mama and Hattie Bea joined the crowd that surrounded Benny in celebration of his team's victory.

"Good game, Benny," Hattie Bea said as their eyes connected through the chaotic scene of hand slaps, and chants on the field.

"That's my son," Mama yelled aloud.

She pointed wildly in Benny's direction as swarms of newspaper reporters shoved to get closer to take pictures and interview Coach Porter and the players.

Benny's eyes met Mama's, but he had no words to respond. He just smiled and nodded his head in agreement.

Mama tried to push her way to get closer to Benny, but she was soon shoved further away by the force of the crowd.

"Alright, baby, you did really good," Mama shouted to Benny as she stretched her arms toward him to give him a hug. "I've gotta go now," she continued, "but I'll see you in a little while," she said with a wink and wave Good Bye.

Benny turned his head and replied, "Sure Mama, as usual, I'll see you later – much later," he repeated under his breath.

He readjusted his damp baseball cap to fit tightly over his forehead as he trotted toward the crowd of his teammates and fans waiting to lift him up on their shoulders and carry him in a victory lap around the field.

Unc and Uncle Bump looked on clapping and cheering along with the crowd.

"Our boy did it," Unc said to Uncle Bump.

"Yeah, he sure did," Uncle Bump agreed as they both enjoyed Benny's moment of victory with pride.

Benny "Cap" Turner
Posing in Cardozo Stadium 1954

CPSIA information can be obtained at www.ICGtesting.com
Printed in the USA
LVOW08s2142180614

390731LV00001B/159/P